# Filthy Doctor

**Filthy, Volume 2**

Amy Brent

Published by Amy Brent, 2021.

This is a work of fiction. Similarities to real people, places, or events are entirely coincidental.

FILTHY DOCTOR

**First edition. March 1, 2021.**



ISBN: 979-8201162887

Written by Amy Brent.

# Also by Amy Brent

**Filthy**

Filthy Boss

Filthy Doctor

Filthy Professor

Filthy Seal

Filthy Cowboy

Filthy Daddy

Filthy Coach

**Forbidded**

The Doctor's Fake Marriage

**Forbidden**

Fake Fiance

One More Chance

Crave Me

My Best Friend's Dad

The Doctor's Fake Marriage

Dad's Best Friend

**Forbidden Fantasies**

Daddy's Business Partner

Daddy's Friend

Daddy O

Climbing His Corporate Ladder

Taken By Daddy's Boss

Filthy Liar

**Standalone**

Teachers' Pet

Filthy Box Set

Knocked Up By My Brother's Best Friend

My Best Friend's Brother

My Best Friend's Ex

Say You're Mine

Club Desire Box Set

My Boyfriend's Dad

Fighting For Her

Forbidden Love Box Set

Love Undercover

Friends With Benefits

A Royal Menage

Baby Fever

Vegas Baby

Brother's Best Friend for Christmas

Christmas With My Best Friend's Dad

My Son's Sitter

Single Dad's Christmas Present

Surrendering To 3 Alphas

Because I Love You
Catching Up With Daddy
Claiming Cinderella
Double Trouble
First Love
First Time
Knocked Up By My Brother's Best Friend
My Best Friend's Boyfriend
Pretend Daddy
Redemption
Roomies With Benefits
Royally Yours
Rub Me The Right Way
Show Stopper
That One Night
The Baby Contract
Truth Or Dare
Santa's Naughty List
Quickie on Christmas
Con Man

# Table of Contents

# FILTHY DOCTOR

by

Amy Brent

This is a work of fiction. While, as in all fiction, the literary perceptions and insights are based on life experiences and conclusions drawn from research, all names, characters, places and specific instances are products of the author's imagination and used fictitiously. No actual reference to any real person, living or dead, is intended or inferred.

**The doctor will see you now... ALL of you.**

I'm a world-renowned cardiologist, but breaking hearts is what I do best.

Women line up for a turn between my Egyptian cotton sheets, making it difficult for me to limit my services to just one.

Well, you can't really blame them.

Because I work hard, REALLY HARD!

With these movie star looks and hands that can work magic - both in the clinic and in the bed, I can make a woman come by just looking at her.

And who wouldn't care about a bank account almost as sizeable as the surgical instrument between my legs.

Life seems to be awesome.

And then Lucy walks back into my world.

We were HOT lovers in high school - and I can remember the night I took her V card.

Now she's back, as the producer of my TV show.

My brain tells me to stop.

But one look into her sultry blue eyes and I wanna go DEEP!

I've learned so many new talents since our last night together,

And I am willing to teach her.

I'm so ready to be her FILTHY DOCTOR.

Her delicious curves tempt me to take her.

I want to own that voluptuous body.

***But doing so would mean risking her career and breaking my biggest rule: Never fall in love.***

# PROLOG

COLE ORDERED THE DRIVER to take us to his penthouse, then raised the tinted glass behind the front seat so we could have a little privacy. We sat in the back seat making out like the two horny teenagers we once were.

His tongue hungrily probed my mouth as his warm hand slipped under my blouse and bra to massage my breast and roll my nipples. Little sparks of electricity shot through my body from head to toe, as if I'd touched an electric fence.

I could feel the intense flood gushing between my legs as my hand slid between his thighs and found his thick cock hard and ready, just like the old days. It felt magical beneath my hand, as if touching it had transported me back in time.

I moaned into his mouth when his hand slid down to my crotch. He rubbed the fabric between my legs until the heat was so intense I thought my slacks might catch fire.

"We're here," he sighed in my ear as the car rolled to a stop in front of his Manhattan penthouse. It was a short ride that ended not a moment too soon. "Let's continue this upstairs."

"Yes, let's," I said, blowing out a long breath and adjusting my blouse as the doorman hurried across the sidewalk to open the car door.

"I have a huge boner," Cole whispered with a boyish grin that I recognized from years ago. He took off his jacket to drape over his arm to cover his protruding cock. He slid out of the car and held out his free hand to me.

When I got out of the car I "accidentally" brushed his cock with my hand. He jumped and I giggled.

"Let's go upstairs and I'll take care of that for you, Dr. Walker," I said. Without another word, he grabbed my hand and literally dragged me inside the building, across the marble foyer, into the gold-paneled elevator, and into his penthouse suite.

We attacked each other the moment the elevator doors closed.

# CHAPTER ONE: Dr. Cole Walker

"YOU FUCKING CARDIOLOGISTS... You all think you're gods or something," Efram said bitterly, albeit it with a smile, as he stared at me from behind the cup of shitty coffee they served in the hospital cafeteria. Dr. Efram Schoenberg was the top anesthesiologist in the city. That's why I brought him in for all my complex operations. Patients who died on the operating table rarely paid their bills. It was Efram's job to keep them breathing while I cut open their chests to repair or replace their hearts. Efram was also one of my best friends and the biggest buster of my balls.

"We don't think we're gods," I said with a smile. I picked up my cup of coffee and held it up in a toast. "Some of us are gods, Efram. And some of us might even be *the* God. So, watch what you say. I'd hate to waste a good lightning bolt on your ass."

"Jesus, how do you carry the weight of that ego?' he asked, rolling his eyes. "It must be a terrible burden."

"It's a burden I willingly bear for the good of mankind," I said with a smile. I tapped my cup to his and settled back in the hard chair to stretch out my legs and let my eyes wander around the room. It was after four in the afternoon, but the Mercy General cafeteria was still bustling with staff and visitors eating the lousy hospital food left over from lunch because it was convenient and relatively cheap. The food was decent if you didn't mind the abundance of grease and salt the kitchen used to give the food a semblance of flavor. I ate there only if I was desperately hungry. Otherwise, I choked down the coffee after long operations with Efram and that was it. I was Dr. Cole Walker, after all. I ate for free at five-star restaurants, not shitty hospital cafeterias.

Efram and I had just come out of a nine-hour heart surgery and admittedly, I was beat. The patient, a fifty-year-old construction worker with total blockage in all three major arteries, was lucky to be alive. Or perhaps I should say that he was lucky that I was in the hospital when the paramedics brought him into the ER after suffering a massive heart attack. No one expected him to live. No one but me, that is. I cracked his chest and manually massaged his heart as he was wheeled into the OR. I stinted his arteries and Efram kept him breathing until I was done. Now he was resting comfortably in ICU. I expected that he'd make a full recovery. How long he would live after that was totally up to him.

Like I said, in this hospital, I was God.

Nobody died on my watch.

Nobody.

If you asked most surgeons what the most difficult part of their job was they wouldn't say that it was replacing a patient's heart or resecting a bowel or reattaching a limb. That stuff a good surgeon could do in his sleep. The most difficult part was standing over a patient for hours at a time as the muscles in your legs and back tied into knots. Most of my peers had back problems after years of hovering over an operating table. I was only thirty-six and in peak physical condition, but today my back was killing me. I needed a nice deep tissue massage, preferably administered by a blonde with big tits and the willingness to finish it off with a happy ending. As if on cue, Monica Craft, one of the scrub nurses I serviced on a regular basis, i.e. fucked whenever the mood struck me, strolled into the cafeteria and headed my way. I could tell she wasn't wearing a bra beneath the pink scrub shirt she wore. And if history was any indication, she wasn't wearing panties either.

"The patient is resting comfortably in recovery," she said, sliding into the chair to my right. She picked up my coffee cup and took a drink, then made a sour face that wrinkled her cute nose. She smacked her lips and grinned me.

"Really?" Efram said, bouncing a frown between us. "Do I need to leave?"

"Nah, you're good," I said, winking at Monica. Efram shook his head and looked away. He knew I fucked Monica on a regular basis and that didn't bother him. He fucked as many nurses as I did. Most doctors did. What bothered him was her air of familiarity. I might have had a God Complex, but Efram had a Class Complex. In his mind, doctors walked among the clouds while nurses, and everyone else, occupied the ground far below. Nurses were beneath doctors, no pun intended. Doctors should not sit or eat or socialize in public with nurses or hospital staff. It was okay for doctors to fuck as many nurses as they pleased, but it was not okay for a nurse to sit down with a doctor in public and sip from his cup. It didn't matter that in a few minutes I'd be fucking Monica's brains out in an empty hospital room or a broom closet.

"It's okay to fuck them," Efram would say. "But don't date them or marry them. And certainly, don't socialize with them in public. It will only cause trouble."

"I'll check on the patient before I leave," I said with a sigh that signaled that I was ready to get the show on the road. I felt my cock twitch in my scrubs as I watched Monica licking the coffee from her lips. She gazed at me with her big blue eyes and let one eyebrow twitch, which was her signal that it was time to play. She was a cute redhead with big tits and thick nipples, and a bush of red curls that proved that the carpet did indeed match the drapes. She was petite and flexible, like a contortionist, and she loved to create new positions. I could literally pick her up and bend her this way and that, or she would climb up me like a kid on a monkey bar and impale her tight pink pussy on my big cock.

Her favorite position was clamping her fingers around my neck while I held on to her ass and swung her into me like a kid on a swing. She was small, but she somehow managed to take most of my ten inches inside her. Monica was a sexual marvel, but Efram was right. I would fuck her till her eyes bugged out behind closed doors, but that was where our relationship ended. Once we left the hospital, there was nothing between us. Monica understood that and said she was fine just having a good time. Besides, she was engaged to a guy who worked in accounting, Bob something or other. She didn't want to marry me, she often said. She just liked fucking doctors.

I was glad Monica knew how the game was played. Again, I was Dr. Cole Walker, the world-renowned cardiologist who literally held life in my hands. I was not only successful and rich, I was also six-foot-two and two hundred pounds of lean muscle, thanks to my daily workouts and five-mile runs.

Call me arrogant, but I pride myself on my looks because they remind me of how far I've come. I was a tall, skinny, awkward kid with big glasses and bad skin. You wouldn't recognize me in my high school yearbook. I blossomed at college, I guess you could say that. It was amazing what getting contacts and clearing up your skin can do for your confidence. I started running and working out and went from being invisible at parties to being the life of them. I went from being invisible to most girls to having my pick of them. Some nights I picked more than one. I fucked sorority girls, teaching assistants, cheerleaders, the little sisters of my frat brothers, and a couple of cougar professors, who taught me how to really please a woman. Ah... good times. I fucking loved college.

Now, I was married to my work, but that didn't stop me from having a very active and very public social life. I had been voted one of New York City's Most Eligible Bachelors five years in a row by *New York Magazine*. I dated high-profile models, actresses, heiresses and socialites, though none seriously. I was in it for the sex and the show, meaning I loved a tight pussy and I loved to show off.

If I was photographed leaving Nobu with a Victoria's Secret model or some hot young actress on my arm, it didn't do anything for my medical career, but it shot my Q-Rating through the roof.

Oh, I should explain what I mean. The Q-Rating is how television networks like World News Network judge how well the audience likes their on-air news talent. The higher the Q-Rating, the more popular the talent. And as I said, my Q-Ratings were through the roof.

What the hell I'm I talking about?

Okay, let me back up.

*World News Network* was a twenty-four-hour cable news channel headquartered in New York City and beamed around the globe. When the mayor had his heart attack two years ago, I was his cardiologist and the one who spoke at subsequent press conferences, giving the status of his health. Ed Quigley, the head of the news division at World News Network saw me and liked my looks and demeanor. As it happened, WNN was looking for a doctor to come on the air every Friday evening and answer medical questions submitted by viewers in a quick segment called "To Your Health". Ed asked me to lunch, pitched me the concept, offered me a fat contract, and voila! The next week, and every Friday since, yours truly has been on TV in front of millions of viewers dispensing sound medical advice with a beaming smile. And building the Q-Rating, which could lead to a lucrative network syndication deal like Dr. Oz or Dr. Phil. Would I leave cardiology to host a TV show? No fucking way. I was a doctor first, a TV star second. However, would I be interested in doing both? Fucking A right, I would.

"So, Dr. Walker," Monica said, giving me a quick sideways glance. She was rubbing her foot up and down the inside of my calf under the table. My cock was already chubbing up. She put her hand on my arm and cooed at me. "Shall we check on that patient?"

"We shall," I said with a smile. The patient's file was on the table. I was glad I'd brought it along. I'd need it to cover the bulge in my scrubs.

I picked up the file and stuck out my right hand to Efram. "Great job keeping the patient asleep, Dr. Schoenberg."

He rolled his eyes at my hand and said, "Whatever."

"Nurse, shall we go?" I pulled out Monica's chair and she somehow managed to brush the back of her hand against my plump cock as she moved past. I looked at Efram and smiled, then let Monica lead the way to whatever spot she had picked out for us to have a little afternoon delight.

# CHAPTER TWO: Lucy Rhodes

"ARE YOU SURE ABOUT this, Lucy? Are you really sure this is the right thing for you to do?"

I could hear my dad's voice in my head as clearly as if he had been standing next to me in the empty New York City apartment that would be my home for the next twelve months. That's how long my new employer World News Network had agreed to pay for housing under my new contract as the executive producer of *WNN'S World News Tonight*. They were paying me a nice salary, but I had heard horror stories about the cost of living in New York City. I didn't know how much the lease payment was on a furnished apartment like this, but I expected that I'd be looking for something smaller and less costly when the year ran out. And that was if I still had the job. I had a one year contract and this was big-time television after all, so nothing was written in stone.

The TV news business was a revolving door. I worked behind the scenes so it was not as cutthroat as being on the air, but I still had to prove my worth to the network or they'd hire someone younger for less money to do the job. And the most difficult part of any executive producer's job, especially at this level, would be dealing with the on-air talent who were usually pompous, egotistical assholes of the male variety, or hot young females who were sleeping or conniving their way to the top. I'd worked at TV stations in little towns and big cities and the one thing they had in common was that they were all soap operas. The only difference were the sizes of the markets and the sizes of the egos. There was no larger market than New York City and I was sure the egos would match.

I smiled when I heard my father's voice in my head, asking if I was sure I was doing the right thing. I'd had a good thing going in Chicago. I had a great job as the executive producer of the nightly news at WCIL, a great house in the suburbs, and what I thought was a great marriage to my college sweetheart, Randy Rhodes, who ended up tearing my world apart and leaving me to sort out the smoldering ruins. Getting the job offer in New York from my old boss, Ed Quigley, was a welcomed coincidence. I jumped at the chance to leave my old life behind and start anew. And now, here I was.

"Are you sure about this, Lucy?" my dad's voice asked again.

"Yes, daddy," I said quietly. "I'm sure." I smiled at the memory of my dad, his soft eyes always so full of concern for his only daughter. I took a deep breath and imagined the smell of his Old Spice and hair cream. I could feel his arms around me, bear hugging me until I grunted while he pretended like he was never going to let me go.

He was always questioning my motives and my decisions when he was alive. It bugged the shit out me when I was a kid, but once I became an adult I understood that most of the questions he asked were submitted for my own wellbeing. It was his way of asking, "Lucy, have you really thought this through? Is this really the right thing for you to do?"

"I have no idea, daddy," I said with a sigh. I shook my head at the meager stack of boxes the moving company had set along the living room wall and gave a heavy sigh. I counted them with my fingers. Ten boxes. I was thirty-four years old and the sad contents of my entire life could be held in ten cardboard boxes with room names scribbled on the side in black marker: KITCHEN. BEDROOM. LIVING ROOM. BATHROOM. MISC.

It was sad to think that this was all I had to show for what I thought was a pretty good life. Sadder still was knowing how quickly that good life could come crashing down when you discovered that your husband was a sex addict with no self-control. Oh, fuck that. I don't believe there's any such thing as a sex addict. Randy was just a guy. He was a self-centered douchebag who thought with his cock rather than his brain. In other words, Randy Rhodes was a typical piece of shit who would fuck anything that moved and some things that didn't. I wasn't sad that I had caught him cheating on me. I was sad that it took ten years of my life to realize what a lowlife piece of shit cocksucker he was.

I'm not bitter.

Oh no, not me...

I met Randy in college. I was the bright-eyed innocent sophomore from Wisconsin and he was the smooth-talking, worldly junior from Chicago who was the life of every party he attended. I met him at a fraternity party and instantly fell in love.

Randy was a marketing major and I was in the journalism program at Stanford. I was a shy, unassuming country girl with blonde curls and timid eyes, and he was the proverbial tall, dark and handsome Italian with coal black hair, deep blue eyes, and a swagger that scared the hell out of me at first, then became a drug I could not resist. I fell madly for him, instantly, without listening to my girlfriends who told me what a pussy hound he was. I made the age-old mistake many women made. I thought I could take a bad boy and change him to suit my needs. I could turn a bad boy good. What a fucking fool I was. It just took me a fucking decade to realize it.

All I knew was that Randy seemed to like me and I damned sure liked him. We made awkward love the night we met in the back seat of his BMW. It wasn't my first time, but it sure felt like it. Maybe it was because I didn't have strong feelings for Randy like I did for my first lover way back in high school. Or maybe it was because Randy was so rough that it hurt when he entered me, so much so that I was afraid to do it with him again. It wasn't that his cock was abnormally large or anything like that. It was just that Randy was a really rough lover. I swallowed my fears and kept fucking him until the roughness and the pain turned to pleasure. I liked rough sex now. No, that's not entirely true. I loved it. I didn't mind a good spanking or a little hair pulling now and then. Hit me in anger and I'll kill you in your sleep. Pull my hair while you're fucking me from behind and I'll gush all over you.

Anyway, Randy and I dated all through college. Being a starry-eyed, smitten girl, I was monogamous from day one, but Randy continued to sow his wild oats. I was okay with it, at least for a while. When I caught him fucking one of my sorority sisters in my bed in my dorm room, that was when I drew the line.

"It's me or them," I said, shaking a finger at him so he couldn't see it trembling from nerves. "I'm not gonna be the girl you come fuck at the end of the night anymore, Randy. I'm done."

"Baby, you know you're the only one that matters," he cooed, pulling me into his arms and rocking me gently against his chest, as if I were a baby that needed comforting.

"Bullshit," I said, pressing my ear to his chest so I could hear his heart beating. I closed my eyes and sighed at the sound.

He stroked my hair and whispered, "Baby, trust me..."

"I mean it," I said, pulling away so suddenly it took us both by surprise. "You can either fuck me or you can fuck them, but you can't fuck us all."

Hearing those words in my head now, seventeen years later, I realized how pathetically stupid they sounded. Who the fuck was I? The Abraham Lincoln of college sex? You can fuck some of the people some of the time...

"I choose you," Randy said convincingly, though in both our hearts we knew it was just more of his bullshit. It just meant that he would be more discriminating as to where he fucked his skanks and I would have to turn a blind eye if I had any hopes of a future with him.

And that was the crazy part. That's when my dad would ask, "Lucy, are you sure about this?" When it came to Randy's vow to be faithful to me, I literally was deaf, dumb, and blind. Even when we both graduated and I followed him to Chicago for work, I knew that I wasn't the only woman in his life. He was very discreet about it, very careful, but I knew about his affairs all the same. And I ignored them. God help me, even when he asked me if I wanted to get married I ignored the fact that he was a cheat.

So, daddy, what was I thinking back then?

To this day, I still had no fucking idea.

Randy was Vice President of Sales for a company that sold microchips to large manufacturers. He made three times what I did as producer of the evening news in Chicago at a mid-ranked station. Everything was in his name because my college loans had maxed my credit. Our house in the suburbs, our cars, his motorcycle that he had never had time to ride, our vacation home in Connecticut, and the boat dry-docked there that had barely been in the water. On paper, it all belonged to him.

I stayed with Randy for thirteen years, then the camel's back finally broke under the weight of a million straws. I came home unexpectedly one afternoon and caught him butt fucking our neighbor Louise on our living room couch. That was it for me. I didn't even scream or throw anything. I opened the door and they both looked up at me in surprise. I gawked at them for a moment, then went upstairs to pack a bag. Randy came bounding up the stairs with the stink of Louise's ass on his cock and her cunt on his breath, pleading with me to listen to reason. I did the only reasonable thing I could think of to do. I kicked him in his dangling ball sack and punched him in the nose with my left hand. The large diamond in my engagement ring went across his face like a can opener, splitting open his cheek and nose with the precision of a paring knife. I quickly packed the rest of my things and left him lying on the bedroom floor clutching his nose with blood running between his fingers. It was one of the most satisfying moments of my life.

"He's going to need stitches, Louise," I said when I reached the bottom of the stairs. She was still standing in the living room clutching her house dress in front of her fat boobs, giving me a horrified look. I smiled at her awkwardness. "Enjoy. He's all yours."

I checked into a hotel and cried myself to sleep. Surprisingly, after the tears ran out I slept like a baby and awoke feeling great, as if a huge weight had been removed from shoulders. As luck would have it, that was the day Ed Quigley called to offer me the job of executive producer at WNN. Ed was my old boss in Chicago. He had been trying to pull me into the big leagues for years. When he asked if I was ready to play in the major leagues, I said yes so fast it made him hesitate.

"Are you serious, Ed?" I asked.

"I am," I said, forcing myself to sound stronger than I felt. "Are you seriously offering?"

"You bet your ass I am," he grunted. Ed was nearing sixty and was as round as he was tall. When he spoke, it was on gusts of breath that seemed to burst from his lungs. "The executive producer of the nightly news is moving on next month. The job is yours if you want it."

"Don't I need to interview first?"

He scoffed. "Not with me. I know how good you are. I trained you, remember? Do you want the job?"

"I want it," I said without hesitation or debate. "Yes. Definitely."

He paused for a moment. Ed knew me well. He had always been like a second father to me. He could tell when something was wrong.

"Is everything okay there, Lucy?" he asked, his voice full of concern. "That dipshit husband of yours giving you trouble?"

"Not anymore," I said with a sigh. "In fact, as soon as I hang up with you I'm calling my attorney. I'm counting on the divorce being quick and painless because I just want out. I'm not going to fight him for anything. He can have it all and I hope it burns down around him."

Ed chuckled. "Hell hath no fury like Lucy Rhodes scorned. Okay, I'll meet with my people today and email an offer to you by the end of the week."

"Thanks, Ed," I said. "Your timing couldn't be better."

“Then that’s good luck for both us,” he said. “I’m glad you’re okay, Lucy. And welcome to the big time.”

# CHAPTER THREE: Cole

"OH, MY GOD... COLE... your cock... is so... fucking big..."

The words gushed out of Monica's moist lips each time I thrust my cock into her. Her pink scrub pants were down around her ankles and the pink scrub shirt was lying on the floor. She was bent over a bathroom sink, clutching onto the sides so tightly that her knuckles were turning white, with her tight, round ass shoved out and my fingers digging into her sides. I was behind her with my knees bent so my cock would line up to her luscious pussy, hammering it to her like there was no tomorrow.

Monica was a small girl and her cunt was so tight it wrapped around my cock like fingers on a hand. She could tense her pussy muscles and squeeze my cock like a milking machine. It was the most amazing thing I'd ever felt, and of course as a medical professional, made me wonder why I hadn't gone into gynecological research. Hmm, maybe I had without even realizing it.

I glanced at her in the mirror over the sink. Her eyes were squeezed shut and her pink mouth was hanging open. Her tongue rolled out and swiped across her lips. Her big milky tits bounced on her chest. I grabbed onto them to keep them still. Her plump nipples caught between my fingers and I gave them a squeeze.

"Fuck... Cole... I'm cumming..." she moaned, getting on her tiptoes and pushing her ass toward me. "Fuck... Cole... cum with me..."

I sucked in a quick breath and tensed every muscle in my body to let my balls know that it was time to blow. I could hold an orgasm with the best of them. When I was young I'd shoot my load even before I got my cock out of my pants. Now, thanks to years of practice with more women that I could count, I could hold off until my partner was ready for me to cum. The only time I didn't hold back was when I was getting my cocked sucked or I was in a hurry. Then, I could come in no time. Why draw it out. It was just a blowjob.

I squeezed Monica's hips and lifted her off the ground, impaling my cock deep inside her until I heard her gasp. I could feel her hot juices gushing out of her pussy around my cock, soaking my balls and filling the tiny bathroom with the pungent aroma of our sex.

"Fuck... meeee... oh... god... I'm...cumming..." Monica started to scream, but I quickly put my hand over her mouth. She bit hard into my fingers and moaned. I somehow managed to keep going as I shot my hot milky load deep inside. When it was over, she pried her teeth from my finger and hung her head, panting like a dog.

"Holy shit, Dr. Walker," she said, looking up at me in the mirror with a sweaty grin on her face. "That was awesome."

"Yes, it was," I said, smiling at her as I stepped back to let my long cock slide from her cunt. She turned around quickly and grabbed my sticky, deflating cock in one hand and put the other hand around my neck. She pulled my lips down to hers and roughly pushed her tongue into my mouth.

"I love your cock," she said, her hand sliding up and down my gooey member. She gave me a pitiful look. "When am I going to get to fuck you outside of this hospital. I mean, this was great, but I have a king-sized bed that would be even better."

"You know the rules," I said, taking her wrist to pull her hand from my cock and gently pushing her away. "If the hospital administrator knew about us, you would lose your job. And your fiancé would shit a brick and call off your wedding. You don't want that to happen."

She leaned her bare ass back against the sink and folded her arms over her tits, which were red and marked from the roughness of our sex. "You keep quoting hospital rules to me. I don't even think there is such a rule. I think you made it up so you wouldn't have to see me outside of the hospital."

"Look it up in the employee handbook," I said with a shrug as I tucked my cock into my shorts and pulled up my black scrubs. "Or go ask your fiancé about it. He works in administration. I'm sure he'd tell you the same thing I'm telling you." I narrowed my eyes to give her a serious look. "I mean, if this isn't enough for you, we can just stop."

"No, this is great," she said quickly, ignoring the fact that we had just fucked in a public restroom the size of a broom closet. It was representative of the nature of our affair. We had fucked in janitor's closets, empty hospital rooms, public restrooms with locks on the doors, bathroom stalls with no locks, unoccupied labs, service elevators, and the laundry room in the basement. We had anointed pretty much every area within the hospital with the sounds and smells of our sex, but we would never meet outside. Monica was a sweet girl and a nice fuck, but she was not someone I'd give the time of day to on the outside. She knew and I knew it, and it wasn't really an issue. Monica always got clingy right after sex.

I nudged her aside and washed my hands while she sat on the toilet and cleaned off her cunt with toilet paper then pulled the pink scrubs back up her legs. I dried my hands on a paper towel and kissed her on the forehead.

"I'm going to check on our patient," I said. "Have a good night. And thanks for this. It was nice."

"You're such an asshole," she huffed, rolling her eyes at me, pretending to be irritated. Then she smiled and kissed me on the cheek. "I'll see you later."

I unlocked the door and stepped out into the brightly-lit hallway. There were three nurses at a station at the end of the hall. They all looked at me, then quickly looked away.

I smiled and headed toward ICU to check on my patient. I could only imagine the gossip that would start when the nurses saw Monica coming out of the bathroom.

The Dr. Cole Walker legend lived on.

# CHAPTER FOUR: Lucy

ED GAVE ME THE GRAND tour of World News Network's news production facilities that took up the entire top three floors of the WNN building located in New Jersey right across the bay from lower Manhattan. I could see the Statue of Liberty from the balcony off the bullpen, where dozens of reporters and writers toiled to produce the network's constant flow of news. Apparently, my morning commute would involve a taxi or subway, and a ferry ride that was pleasant in the spring and fall, but hot as fuck in the summer and cold as a witch's tit in winter. Those were Ed's words, not mine.

"If you're here next year think about moving over to this side of the bay," Ed said as I followed him into his office. He directed me toward a chair and he slid in behind his desk. His belly pushed against the desk, so he pushed his chair back.

"If I'm here next year?" I said, giving him the eye. "You think I'll be burnt out by then? Or fired?"

Ed smiled and his eyes nearly disappeared above his puffy cheeks. He had gotten even rounder since I'd seen him last. He grunted when he moved and sweated a lot. His once red hair had turned gray and was cut into an old-fashioned crew cut. He tugged a Kleenex from a box on the desk and mopped his face with it.

"This place will burn anybody out," he said with a heavy sigh. "Look at me. I'm only thirty years old."

"You don't look a day over fifty-nine," I said with a smile. "I appreciate you giving me this chance, Ed. I won't let you down."

"I know you won't," he said, waving the tissue at me. "If you're still the hungry go-getter I hired in Chicago all those years ago, you'll do fine here. The audience and the egos are bigger, otherwise, it's all the same."

"When do I get to meet my anchors and staff?" I asked, glancing at the large photographs on his wall of the network stars under Ed's control. The main anchors for WNN's Nightly News were Bryant Hart and Stephanie Bean. I'd seen them countless times on TV but had not had the chance to meet them yet.

Bryant was a youthful-looking fifty-something with perfect gray hair and perfect teeth and steel blue eyes that cut into the camera like lasers. He had been the network's star for twenty years and showed no signs of stopping. Stephanie Bean was probably his tenth co-anchor. It was common knowledge in the industry that Bryant was a bitch to work with and she was just the latest in a long line of comers.

Stephanie was in her early thirties but tried to sell it as late twenties. She was a drop dead gorgeous blonde, a former Miss Kentucky, who had come out of journalism school full of talent and drive and reportedly fucked, clawed and backstabbed her way to the network chair. These were my two stars that worked for me, at least during the hour when I was in the booth controlling the show.

"Let me give you a little insight on your anchors," Ed said quietly, even though the office door was shut. "Bryant Hart is an egotistical pussy hound that's probably fucked most of the women worth fucking in the place and will try to fuck you."

"Define 'worth fucking,'" I said with a smile. "And should I be flattered that I'm included in that club?"

"You know what I mean," Ed said, huffing, shaking his head. "He's like most male anchors. He thinks he's a bigger star than he is, though Bryant's numbers are pretty damn good and have been for a long time. Good enough to make him the number two anchorman on cable."

"And what about Miss Kentucky?" I asked, nodding at her picture. She really was gorgeous, with her big blonde hair and infectious smile and a pair of legs reportedly insured for a million dollars. "What's her story?"

Ed leaned back in the chair and laced his fingers over his round belly. "Stephanie is a piece of work. Q-Ratings are off the chart with men. Not so much with women, which is why we paired her with Bryant. She is bright, talented, smart, and will probably be our sole anchor if she hangs around long enough for Bryant to either retire or drop dead of a heart attack in a strip bar. She is also conniving, ruthless, self-serving, and the most narcissistic person you will ever meet. You will either love or hate her immediately and the feeling will be mutual, I guarantee."

"Lovely," I said. "So, I have two anchors with two huge egos to contend with. Anyone else I need to be warned about? What about the sports guy and the weatherman?"

Ed smiled and shook his head. "Both easily managed because they're not that smart," Ed said. He wagged a finger at the anchor's pictures on the wall. "Nope, these are the Medusas of the bunch. Everyone else, reporters, producers, writers, tech, directors, assistants, are easy as pie to manage compared to those two."

"That's good to know," I said with a nod. "So, if everyone understands that when it comes to producing the show, I'm in charge, we should have no problems."

"You will have no problem there," he said, his round head bobbing as if the muscles in his neck were giving out. "Even those with the biggest egos understand that the show comes first. They want every newscast to be the best it can be. And if anyone gives you shit," he said, grinning at me, "I'm sure you'll be able to handle it without running to me."

I smiled. "I think I'll be fine."

"Oh, one more thing," he said, leaning forward with his elbows planted on the desk. "Dr. Cole Walker is coming in for a meeting later today. I'd like you to be on hand."

"Dr. Cole Walker?" I vaguely knew the name, but couldn't put a face to it. "Who is he?"

"Dr. Walker is one of the world's foremost cardiologists," Ed said proudly, as if he were talking about one of his kids. He started moving folders around on the desk, looking for something. "I thought I had his bio and headshot here somewhere."

"Why would a cardiologist have a bio and headshot?" I asked.

He gave up the search and laced his fingers together on the desk like he needed to keep his hands busy. "Walker has done a medical segment for us every Friday for the last year or so. He comes on set with Bryant and Stephanie and answers a medical question from a viewer. I'm pretty sure that Stephanie is giving him a hand job under the desk. He's that goddamn good looking."

"Okay, so why is he coming in for a meeting?"

"Because his Q-Ratings are off the fucking charts," Ed said, looking for the folder again. "The audience loves him. The powers that be upstairs who keep up with such things think we need to give him a longer segment or put him on twice a week. And there's talk of even giving him his own show." He shook his head as if he were respectful of the guy's talent. It was something I'd rarely seen Ed do. "The guy could be the next Dr. Oz, if Dr. Oz looked like Ben Affleck in his prime."

"Well, I can't wait to meet him," I said. "What time?"

"Around three. I'll page you when he gets here."

"Sounds great," I said with a sigh. I glanced at my watch. It was almost one. Ed had scheduled an all-hands meeting to introduce me to my new crew.

He saw me glance at my watch and realized the time. "So, you ready to meet your staff?"

"I am." I patted my thighs as if I was beating a drum, and got to my feet.

"Okay, let's go." He huffed as he pushed himself out of the chair and moved around the desk. He started to open the door, then paused to give me a serious look. "Fair warning, Lucy, this ain't Chicago."

"What does that mean?" I asked.

"It means this ain't a local station and you're not producing the local news. Our signal goes around the world. We compete directly with CNN and Fox News. If you thought Chicago was cutthroat, you ain't seen nothing yet."

"A bit of a lion's den?"

"That's putting it mildly," he said. "You can handle them, just keep your claws out and don't be afraid to use your teeth."

"Can I use them on Bryant if he tries to get fresh with me?"

Ed smiled. "Sure, just don't scratch him so it shows on the air."

I FOLLOWED ED TO THE elevator and up a floor, then through the center of a large room lined with desks where several dozen people sat pecking away at computer terminals or talking on the phone. There were big screen monitors mounted from the ceiling along one wall, one for each of the seven major news networks: CBS, NBC, ABC, CNN, Fox News, MSNBC, and HLN. They were all on with the sound turned down.

"This is the news bay," Ed said as we walked, sweeping a hand through the air like he was spreading pixie dust. "This is where all the writers, researchers, fact checkers, assistant producers, and everyone else sits. Your office is in the far corner next to the conference room."

I followed the point of his finger to a corner office that was separated from the open bay by a glass wall and sliding door. "Not much privacy," I said.

"There is no such thing as privacy here," he said, grinning at me from over his shoulder. "Give these people a closed door and there's no telling what they might do."

"What does that mean?" I asked, having to walk quickly to keep up. I heard him chuckle, but he didn't answer the question.

"The studio and control room are one floor up," he said, one pudgy finger pointing toward the ceiling. "I'll take you up there after you meet your anchors and crew."

According to Ed, seventy-eight people worked behind the scenes, in the field, and on camera to produce the Monday through Friday evening broadcasts of WNN's *World News Tonight.* We would be meeting with the twenty or so department managers and directors. Everyone organizationally reported to Ed, the head of the news division and acting news director, but I was completely in charge of what went on the air every night, and during that one hour, I was God. His words, not mine, though I liked the sound of them just fine.

Ed led me into a large conference room where twenty people sat around a long table and in chairs lined up against the walls. I recognized my stars immediately. Bryant Hart sat at the end of the table, looking like he just fell out of a Land's End catalog with his perfect gray hair and steel blue eyes. He was immaculately dressed in an expensive suit. When our eyes met, he gave me a little nod but kept his expression blank. His co-anchor and the rising star of the show, Stephanie Bean, sat to Bryant's right. She was even more beautiful in person than on TV or in photographs. Her hair and makeup were perfect. Her green eyes sparkled when she looked at me. She gave me a smile that hugged me like a warm blanket. It was no wonder *World News Tonight* had more male viewers than female. Stephanie was like a magnet. You couldn't help but stare at her. Still, given Ed's warnings, I knew there was more behind the polite smile than met the eye. She was ruthless and ambitious, not afraid to fight or fuck her way up the ladder. I knew that we would either be best friends or the worst of enemies. I'd let her decide which one.

"Okay, folks, thanks for coming," Ed said, standing at the head of the table with his hands up. He gave them a minute to direct their attention to the front of the room, where I stood behind him like a timid little girl on the first day of class. I took a deep breath and stepped up beside him, forcing myself to act like the strong leader I'd been hired to be.

"This is Lucy Rhodes, our new executive producer of the weeknight newscasts," Ed said proudly, turning to put a pudgy hand on my shoulder. "Lucy comes to us by way of Milwaukee and Chicago where she worked as the producer of their nightly newscasts for the last ten years. She worked for me when I ran things in Chicago so you know she's top notch. She wouldn't be here if she wasn't." He turned to me and pushed his bushy eyebrows up. "Lucy, they're all yours."

"Thanks for that warm introduction, Ed," I said with a smile. Ed gave me a nod and stepped aside. I saw Bryant and Stephanie exchange a quick glance. Everyone else was looking at me with eyes wide, as if they were wondering what to expect. The people in the room were the heads of the various departments that worked together to produce the news: video editors, directors, camera ops, assignment editors, reporters, technicians, etc. Ed managed them directly and they managed their people, but as the executive director of the show, they also unofficially worked for me. In a perfect world, things should run smoothly. I'd been in the business long enough to know that that was rarely the case.

I clasped my hands together like a teacher on the first day of school and let my eyes go around the room. "Well, it's nice to be here and I look forward to the great work we're going to do together. Why don't we start by going around the room so you can tell me your name and what you do here."

"Bryant Hart, lead anchor," Bryant said in his deep TV voice, interrupting my intention to start with the person sitting closest to me. He pushed himself out of the chair and stood tall adjusting his cufflinks. "And I have better things to do than attending a meet and greet." He walked around the table and out the door. Ed looked at me and rolled his eyes.

"Stephanie Bean, co-anchor," Stephanie said without getting up. She looked toward the door and rolled her eyes. "Don't pay any attention to him. Meetings are actually much nicer after he's left the room. The air is much less stifling."

Everyone chuckled and nodded in agreement. I looked at Stephanie and smiled. We might not become the best of friends, but I had to admire the size of her balls. I held out my hands and said, "Okay, let's continue."

# CHAPTER FIVE: Cole

I'M PROBABLY ONE OF the few doctors in the world who has a team of managers and agents working constantly to guide their career outside of the operating room. I've got a three-book deal with Harper Collins, even though I've never written a book in my life and have no idea what to write about. According to Stan Freeman, my literary agent, they just wanted to tie up the rights to any book I might one day write, and pay me half a million bucks to do so. Sweet. Maybe someday they'll get something for their money. Until then, bank that bitch!

I also have an entertainment lawyer who acts as my agent for the TV work I do. Ben Wolf is his name, which was an appropriate name given his ability to rip people to shreds in negotiations. He was the guy who negotiated my original deal with World News Network and was working on my contract renewal.

I'd been the Friday medical expert on World News Tonight for twelve months now and my contract was about to expire. They paid me a shit ton of money just to show up every Friday at 6:15 and talk for two minutes. I'd never done the math, but I think it came out to something like $2,000 a minute. Fuck, I didn't even earn that much operating on a heart. Not too shabby for a country boy from Wisconsin, if I do say so myself. It was the exposure I got from doing the spots for the news that got me the other deals that were now in play. Along with the books, I got paid to do corporate speaking, I was starting a podcast (whatever the fuck that is), my private practice fees were double what they were a year ago, and if all went according to plan, this time next year I'd have my own syndicated TV show. Move over Dr. Oz. Dr. Cole Walker is coming through!

"So, what do you think?"

My thoughts were interrupted by Ben Wolf's gruff voice coming over the speaker phone in the back of the limo that was driving me to my meeting with Ed Quigley at WNN.

"What do I think about what?" I asked.

"Jesus, are you not listening?"

"I'm listening," I said with a smile. "But repeat it anyway."

"Your contract with WNN comes up for renewal in two weeks," Ben said. "I'm going to propose that they double the rate they're paying you now and book you for longer segments. They must know that we're talking to Kingston World about a one-hour show. We have them over a barrel and can dictate terms."

"So why are we just doubling the rate?" I asked, glancing out the tinted window at the city that was rushing by. I gave him a bored sigh. "I mean, if I'm worth double, I must be worth quadruple, don't you think?"

"Well, maybe..."

"Ben, don't lose your balls now," I said firmly. "Quadruple the rate, expand the Friday segment to three minutes, and get me a thirty-minute special every few months, my time permitting. That is until we can lock down a syndication deal with Kingston or whomever, then all bets are off."

"You want an out-clause in case the syndication deal comes through?"

Of course," I huffed. "I'm not going to show up there every Friday to do a segment when I have a show of my own to focus on. Include the out-clause, end of discussion."

"And if they don't agree?"

"Fuck 'em," I said with a smile. "We'll go to Fox."

"Okay, that's what I'll pitch," he said. "Are you on your way to meet Ed and the new executive producer? I'll wait to see how that goes before I call the head of programming with our new terms."

"I am on my way to meet with them now." I peered out the front window. "I'm ten minutes out. What do you know about the new executive producer?"

"Not much. Worked in Milwaukee for a few years, your old stomping ground, then produced the nightly news for a station in Chicago for the last ten years. She was Ed Quigley's protégé right out of college. Name is... hang on... Lucinda Rhodes. She's female, so that works in your favor."

"Lucinda Rhodes," I said with a smile. "Okay, Ben. I'll keep you posted. And Ben, don't let me down."

"Don't worry, Calvin. I've got this."

I smiled. Ben was the only person on the planet allowed to call me Calvin. And he knew better than to ever do so in public. Calvin was a name I hadn't used in years because it reminded me of a skinny kid from Wisconsin who had few friends and fewer prospects.

I'd left Calvin Colton Walker behind years ago.

Now I was Dr. Cole Walker.

And I was the fucking king of the world.

# CHAPTER SIX: Lucy

ED AND I WERE SITTING in his office waiting for Dr. Cole Walker to arrive. Our meeting was set for three o'clock. It was now three-fifteen and Walker had yet to show. Ed didn't seem too concerned or too pissed off, which again, was totally out of character for him. He busied himself with answering emails and talking to his wife on the phone about the grandkids coming to visit next weekend. I got the impression that the good doctor operated on his own schedule, no pun intended. Still, Ed was usually a pit bull when it came to keeping a tight schedule. This guy must be something if Ed was willing to just hang out and wait for him.

"Okay, when Dr. Walker gets here don't look directly into his eyes for more than a few seconds," Ed said as he turned from the computer to face me. He put his hands behind his head and began to rock. He had a serious frown on his face.

I frowned back. "What does that mean?"

"It means that he has a way of hypnotizing women. Damnedest thing I've ever seen."

"You make him sound like a vampire," I said with a smile. "Or a mad dog."

"Take your pick," he said with a shrug. "I'm just warning you, he has this way about him. Christ, I'm sure Stephanie must change her panties every time he's on set. Even Bryant seems in awe of the guy. He freakin' gushes over him. Again, the damnedest thing I've ever seen."

"I'm sure I'll be fine," I said with a mock frown. "Trust me. Men have very little effect on me these days. Other than to piss me off."

"Speaking of men pissing you off, when's the last time you heard from your asshole ex-husband?" Ed had known Randy from our days back in Chicago. He was at our wedding. He didn't care for Randy then and certainly didn't have much use for him now.

"I haven't talked to Randy since I left Chicago," I said. I felt the muscles in my cheeks tighten at the mention of his name. "There's really nothing left to say."

Ed was about to say something, then he glanced past me at the open doorway and smiled, which was odd because Ed never smiled. He pushed himself up from the chair and went around the desk. I turned to see who he was looking at and came eye to eye with the most gorgeous man I'd ever seen. At least the most gorgeous man that I'd ever seen in person.

The man standing in the doorway was tall, with jet black hair and baby blue eyes and teeth so perfect and white they almost didn't look real. He had a deep tan and a Kennedy jawline. He was wearing a dark suit that probably cost more than my first car, an open-collared white shirt that showed off tufts of dark curls on his chest, and a gold Rolex that looked like it weighed twenty pounds on his wrist. When he looked at me and smiled I literally thought I was going to melt in my panties. The last time my pussy felt this hot I had accidentally sat on a black bicycle seat that had been out in the summer sun all day long.

"Hey, there he is," Ed said happily, sticking out his hand and patting Dr. Cole Walker on the shoulder. "How are you doing, doc?"

"I'm fine, Ed, thank you," Walker said formally. I swallowed the lump that had lodged in my throat and clasped my hands together behind me. I tried not to bounce on the balls of my feet like a love struck high school girl... high school... That's when it hit me. Holy shit. I knew Dr. Cole Walker from another life, from another time. Holy shit...

"Lucy? Oh, my god, Lucy Walsh? Is that you?"

He let go of Ed's hand and moved toward me with his arms outstretched and a look of wonder on his handsome face. I stood dumbfounded as he wrapped his strong arms around me and pulled me in for a hug. He squeezed me tight and grunted playfully, then pulled back with his hands on my shoulders. His eyes went around my face.

He said, "My god, Lucy, I can't believe it's you."

"You two know each other?" Ed asked, his bushy eyebrows in a deep vee above his eyes. "Stupid question, obviously, you do."

"We do know each other," Cole said, eyes sparkling. "Or we did. We were high school sweethearts." He gave me a big grin. "You look like you've seen a ghost, Lucy."

I think my mouth moved for several seconds before my brain decided to take part in the conversation. I blinked away the shock and mustered a smile.

I muttered, "Calvin Walker? From Milwaukee? You're Dr. Cole Walker?"

"Colton is my middle name," he said, nodding. "Cole sounds so much better than Calvin, don't you think?" He glanced over at Ed and made a mock serious face. "If you tell anyone my name is Calvin I'll have to kill you."

"No worries there, doc," Ed said with a smile, his pudgy hands waving in the air. He put his fingers to his lips and pretended to turn the key. "Your secret's safe with me."

I was smiling, too, because I'd never seen Ed so openly enamored of anyone. But I couldn't blame him. Gazing into Dr. Cole Walker's eyes it was easy to see how anyone could fall in love with him, even a fat sixty-year-old heterosexual man who was normally as affectionate as a rattlesnake. It was no wonder the viewers loved him.

Without thinking, I wrapped my arms around his waist and melted into him again. He laughed as he put his arms around me and made cute little grunting noises as he rocked me from side to side. I put my head on his chest and sighed. I could only imagine what Ed was thinking. Heck, I could only imagine what Calvin—I mean—Cole was thinking, being accosted by a woman he hadn't seen in nearly twenty years like some deranged fan.

It felt like old times, only I was hugging the famous Dr. Cole Walker and not nerdy Calvin Walker, the skinny, teenage boy who took my virginity in exchange for his.

# CHAPTER SEVEN: Lucy

I HATED HIGH SCHOOL. My mother literally had to pry me out of bed in the morning to get me to go, I hated it so much. I was an awkward girl with unruly blonde hair and pimples and skinny legs and practically no boobs or hips (those came later, thank God).

There was nothing round about me other than my IQ, which was around 130. I was gifted, but was certainly no genius, at least when it came to being social or attracting boys. I was easily the smartest girl in the eleventh grade, which wasn't that surprising given that most of the other girls were focusing all their time and limited brain cells on their wardrobe and makeup; and on creative ways to lose their virginity. I was the least sexual girl in all of Milwaukee. All my vagina was good for was getting stuck to my panties during sweaty gym classes.

I was probably the only girl in the eleventh grade not having sex of some kind. I remember a contest among the eleventh-grade girls as to who could have sex with the most varsity football players. Hand jobs counted as one point, blowjobs counted as two, and if you went all the way, that was three. And if you let him stick it in your ass (ouch!!), that would get you two bonus points. Points were tallied at the end of the semester and the lucky winner got the title of Biggest Slut—slash—Biggest Athletic Supporter in the school, which was on par with being crowned prom queen at my school. Needless to say, I did not participate. I barely knew what a penis was, and the thought of having one in my mouth just grossed me out. God forbid one ever try to invade my vagina or butt hole!

The school work was easy for me mainly because I gave a damn. While my peers were out cheerleading or painting posters for the big game or getting laid in the back of some football player's car, I was locked in my room studying. Academically, I would accept nothing but the absolute best. I once argued with a teacher who had given me a 99 on an exam when I felt I deserved 100. After an hour, I wore him down and he changed my grade. I earned that 100. I deserved it. I didn't put much thought into my looks, but I'd be damned if some old fart with thinning hair and thick glasses was going to ruin my perfect grade point for the year.

I had one friend, a girl named Wanda Couric, who was as big a nerd as me. We never went to high school dances or football games because we thought sports were too violent and high school boys too stupid. Such thought processes made for a lot of lonely Saturday nights. After a while, we even got tired of each other's company. You can only go to a pity party so many times before even that gets old. Wanda ended up getting contacts and wearing short skirts and joined the in-crowd while I just kept slogging along with my eye toward college. High school was like a prison to me. One more year and I would be paroled. It didn't occur to me at the time that college was going to be ten times worse.

Then, toward the end of my junior year, Calvin Walker transferred to Milwaukee High and my entire world flipped upside down. He was an Army brat whose family moved every couple of years. I vividly remembered the first time I saw him. It was a Friday after lunch, in the middle of Mrs. Higgins' advanced calculus class. I was in my seat at the front where I always sat. The door opened and this tall, skinny boy with a shock of jet black hair hanging in his eyes and glasses with thick frames walked in. He handed Mrs. Higgins a note from the office and stared at the floor. She turned to the class to announce him, as if anyone but me even cared. Most of the kids didn't even look up.

"Class, this is... Calvin Walker... a transfer student from... oh goodness... Berlin, Germany. Are you German, Calvin?"

He shook his head without looking up or saying anything. She gave him a smile full of pity because she knew what a snake pit Milwaukee High could be, especially if you were a nerdy kid with no social skills, as he appeared to be. She patted his shoulder and told him to find a seat. The only seat available was the one at the very front of the row to my right. I watched him out of the corner of my eye as he folded his long legs into the seat and laced his long fingers together on the desk. He sat down without looking around, almost as if he were afraid to see what was around him.

Calvin Walker was tall and lanky, with not much meat on his bones. His chin was dotted with pimples and he had a few dark hairs shadowing his upper lip. When he sensed that I was staring at him he glanced over and gave me a quick, nervous smile, as if he was glad to find someone here even more of a nerd than he was. What struck me most about him was the color his eyes behind the thick lenses. They were bright blue, like the sky on a clear summer's day. There was something about the way he smiled at me that made me all warm and fuzzy inside. I knew at that moment that Calvin Walker and I were going to be the best of friends. Maybe even more.

I got up the nerve to approach him in the lunchroom the next day. He was sitting alone at a table by the window, picking at a piece of meatloaf with the tines of a fork as if he were trying to figure out exactly what it was made of. I usually ate alone, but that day I slid onto the round plastic seat directly across from him without asking permission and just started talking. It was greatly out of character for me, but there was something about Calvin even then that drew me to him, like a moth drawn to a flame. Granted, it was a nerdy flame, but a flame nevertheless.

"Hi there," I said brightly. I had never flirted before a day in my life, so I had no idea how to go about it. And looking seductive was not in my bag of tricks, so I just smiled to show him the perfect teeth that had only been free of braces for a few weeks and stuck out my hand. "I'm Lucy. Lucy Walsh."

He wiped his mouth off on the back of his left hand and shook my hand with his right. His grip was limp, as if he were afraid of squeezing too tightly. "Calvin Walker." He said it in such a way that it sounded like he was asking me if Calvin Walker was his name rather than telling me that it was.

"Hi, Calvin Walker," I said, giving his hand a good shake to let him know that I wasn't going to break. "Walsh and Walker... Walker and Walsh... I bet we're next to each other in the yearbook!" It was a retarded thing to say and I immediately regretted it, but he smiled and bobbed his head. His hand was warm and moist. I pulled my hand back and rubbed my palms on the legs of my jeans for a moment, then fiddled with opening the container of milk on my lunch tray. "So, where are you from?"

"All over the place," he said in the questioning tone again. "We just moved here from Berlin."

"Berlin? Wow. How cool was that? Living in Germany?"

"Not very," he said with a shrug.

I took a sip of the cold milk and picked up my fork. I had a lump of meatloaf on my tray, as well, along with a scoop of mashed potatoes and a few green beans. I dipped the fork into the potatoes and carefully stuck it in my mouth, being as ladylike as possible. My mom always told me to eat sparingly around boys. Take small bites, don't eat everything. "You don't want them to think you're a pig, dear," she would say.

I daintily wiped my lips on a napkin and kept prying. "So, what brings you to Milwaukee, Calvin Walker?"

"My dad's in the Army," he said with a heavy sigh, as if the weight of traveling the world was pressing down upon him. "He's just got transferred to Fort McCoy in Monroe, so we'll be here for a year or two."

"Do you like it so far?"

"I'm not sure yet," he said, narrowing his eyes to look around the lunchroom for a moment. The place was a haven for cliques. The jocks were at one table. The cheerleaders at another. The remainder of the tables were divided among groups of popular kids, unpopular kids (who weren't even popular amongst themselves), the brainiacs, the dopers, the drunks, the criminals, and others who ate lunch in their own little worlds, trying to avoid the real world around them. *Just let me get through the day without getting the shit kicked out of me,* they prayed. I had to admit that I had days like that, where I hunkered down in my own little world and tried to go unnoticed. Being smart didn't score you points in high school. To the contrary, the smart kids were usually the most alienated and bullied because they made the popular kids and the jocks feel stupid. They felt stupid because that's what they were, stupid, not because someone else made them feel that way.

When his eyes came back to mine, he smiled just enough to let me know that he was glad I was there. "Other than the food, I think it's going to be okay."

"I think so, too," I said happily. I grinned at him and he grinned back at me, and without another word, our bond was formed.

From that day forward, Calvin and I had lunch together every day and hung out just about every weekend. We discovered a mutual love of advanced math (nerds), competitive chess (nerds again), and a fascination with all things *Star Wars*. After school, we'd meet at the library so I could help him catch up on his studies. Schools in Germany were a world apart from good old Milwaukee High. Calvin was smart, maybe smarter than me, but he needed a little extra tutoring and I was happy to help.

I remembered sitting next to him at a table in the library, our chairs so close that our thighs touched. A little tingle ran up my leg into my vagina, which had never seen an object more foreign than a bar of soap and the monthly supply of tampons. My clit tingled when his hand accidentally brushed mine. When I got home from the library some days I had to change my panties because the crotch would be soaked. Calvin was waking something up in me that I knew had always been there but had never tried to come out before. I wondered if I had the same effect on him. I decided that the next time we were alone, I'd somehow manage to accidentally brush against his crotch to see if his penis was hard. It funny how ridiculously clinical I sounded back then. *I wanted to see if his "penis was hard".* I was sixteen, for Pete sake. I had no idea what to call a boy's thing back then. If a boy had told me he wanted to shove his throbbing cock into my tight teen pussy I would have run away screaming. Now... well... not so much.

A few weeks later, Calvin came to my house after school to study. We were in my room with the door open (there were no rules governing the doors in my house because a boy had never set foot there), sitting on the floor with our knees touching and our calculus books open on our laps when my mom stuck her head in to say that she was running to the grocery store. It would be hours before my dad would be home and she had to get something for dinner. She asked Calvin if he'd like to stay for dinner and he said sure. I waited until I heard the front door close and the car pull away, then I put my book aside and leaned forward to kiss Calvin on the lips. The look of shock on his face was priceless.

"What are you doing?" he asked, pulling his head back.

"I'm kissing you, dummy," I said. I was on my knees in front of him, which my hands resting on his knees. I tried to work up a seductive look. "Is that all right?"

I saw his Adam's apple bob as he swallowed hard. "Sure..."

I leaned in and kissed him again. This time he kissed me back. I pushed the book off his lap and put my hands on his shoulders to push him back to lie flat on the floor. With him on his back, I straddled his hips and pushed my crotch against him. With my lips still on his and my tongue awkwardly in his mouth, I felt his cock getting hard beneath me. And I mean rock hard and huge, like straddling the bar on a boy's bike.

"Does that feel good?" I asked, rubbing myself against him.

"Yes..." he whispered with his eyes closed. He slid his hands up my thighs and brought them around to my ass. He dug in his fingers and pressed me to him.

The pressure of my pussy against his cock made me tingle all inside. I took a deep breath and moaned in his ear. "Oh... wow... that feels... really good..."

I had never French kissed before, but I was glad to see that it wasn't hard to figure out. Calvin's tongue came out to play with mine. His hands on my ass got firmer and he ground my pussy against his cock. I was wearing jeans and cotton panties, which were drenched from the waves of juices that were gushing from deep inside me. The fabric between us was hot from the friction. I could just imagine us catching fire and the Milwaukee Fire Department having to come put us out.

I heard Calvin gasp and he pressed me to his cock and lifted his ass off the floor. I didn't realize it at that moment, but he was cumming in his jeans. At first, I thought he was in pain, but when I pulled back from his lips I saw the look of teen ecstasy on his face. His eyes were closed behind the thick glasses. His mouth was hanging open and he was sucking in quick gasps of air. I felt him growing hot beneath me as his milky goo soaked the front of his jeans. I could smell our sex in the air; pungent, tangy, intoxicating.

When it was over, his face turned red from embarrassment and the mood suddenly changed. I climbed off him and looked at the wet spot on the front of his jeans. I hid a smile behind my hand and quickly looked away. I was proud of myself because I made that happen. It was the first time I realized that I could pleasure a boy and get pleasure in return. It sparked something inside of me. I wanted to do it again. I wanted to do more, other things, nasty things. I wanted to do everything the sluts at school talked about.

"Uh, I gotta go," he said as his face turned ten shades of red. He stumbled to his feet and gathered up his books. "I'll... I'll see you later."

He covered his crotch with the books and hurriedly left the room. I sat there for a moment in my soggy panties with my clit tingling and my pussy dripping, unsure what to do next. I knew nothing about masturbation back then, so I was left high and dry, or high and wet, so to speak.

If that happened today, I'd just pull out my little box of toys I kept in my bedside table and give myself a happy ending. But I was just sixteen and that was my first foray into sex, if you could even call it that.

Eventually, I just got up and went into the bathroom to clean myself off. I put on clean panties and jeans and went back to my studies, all the while thinking that the next time this happened we'd both leave satisfied.

# CHAPTER EIGHT: Cole

WHEN I WALKED INTO Ed Quigley's office and saw Lucy Walsh standing there, I literally felt my heart clench in my chest, like fingers had closed around it to give it a tight squeeze. I had no idea that World News Tonight's new executive producer Lucinda Rhodes would turn out to be Lucy Walsh, the first girl I had ever had sex with. And the first girl I ever loved. Hell, she might have been the only girl I'd ever really loved. It had been nearly twenty years since I'd seen her, but I'd never even come close to the kind of relationship I had with Lucy. Some would call that sad. I just called it life. I had been too wrapped up in my career to even think about a serious relationship. Plus, I had too much fun playing the field. What was the old saying? Why buy the cow when you can get the milk for free? In my case, it was why buy the cow when you already had access to an entire dairy farm. I had all the free milk I could drink. Hell, I could bathe in free milk. Why fuck that up with silly things like monogamy and commitment?

As Lucy and I stood there locked in a hug, Ed stared at us like a man witnessing an alien landing. He wasn't quite sure what was going on, but he hoped it was a good thing. When Lucy and I finally pulled away from each other, Ed directed us to sit in the two chairs across from his desk while he got us all coffee. Lucy and I sat down and stared into each other's eyes. It was clear that we were thrilled to see each other, but neither of us knew what to say, so we just stared at each other.

Time had been wonderful to Lucy. The last time I'd seen her she was a skinny teenage girl with unruly blond curls and little boobs and practically no ass. Now, eighteen years later, she was strikingly beautiful even though her face bore very little makeup and her hair was pulled up into a thick ponytail at the crown of her head. She still had the freckles dotting her nose and the big smile full of perfect teeth. And her body had matured wonderfully. As we hugged, I could feel her breasts pressed against me and when my hands slid down the small of her back they stopped at the top of her round ass. I had to resist the urge to press my cock against her. I wouldn't have been embarrassed, but Lucy might have and good old would have for sure.

We were turned sideways in the chairs just looking at each other without speaking, letting our eyes catch up with the years. As I gazed into her blue eyes my mind drifted back in time, to the night that we popped each other's cherries in the back seat of my dad's car. Christ, if I knew then what I know now, it wouldn't have been so awkward or over so quickly.

We had been sweethearts for months before the night we finally went all the way, although I couldn't recall that we'd ever made our relationship official by branding ourselves as going steady. I mean, I had never formally asked her to be my girlfriend and she never referred to me as her boyfriend. We just were...

We had initially bonded over our nerdiness, then the sex came later. We were both smarter than the other students at Shitwaukee High. She was exceptionally good at math and I was a whiz in science, we liked to play hours of speed-chess, and watch *Star Wars* movies. We spent a lot of time together, but I had to admit, I was not the one who took our relationship to the next level. She made the first move one day while we were studying in her bedroom. You must understand that I was your average teenage boy with raging hormones. That meant that I thought about sex all the time and would get huge boners that just popped up out of nowhere and wouldn't go away at the worst of times. I spent much of my time praying the hard on in my jeans would go down before the bell rang or before my dad told me to get up and clear the dinner dishes. Even before my initial encounter with Lucy, when I shot my load in my jeans while she rubbed her hot crotch against me, sex was all that I could think about. Thankfully, Lucy seemed to be as obsessed with my cock and balls as I was with her pussy and tits.

We couldn't keep our hands and mouths off each other after that day. A few days after our first encounter, Lucy let me feel her tits and pussy through her clothes. I would rub her jeans until the material was hot as lava beneath my fingers, but I wouldn't stop until she squeezed my hand between her thighs and made this little mewing sound to let me know that she was cumming. I gladly let her rub my cock until I shot off in my jeans, hoping that soon she would let me take it out so she could handle it for real. I longed to have her fingers and mouth on my cock. And my cock buried deep inside her pussy. Funny, my mom wondered why I'd started doing my own laundry all of a sudden. I told her that I just wanted to help her out around the house. My old man knew better. He was an Army Ranger who bragged that he had lost his virginity when he was fourteen to my Aunt Becky's best friend, who was sixteen at the time. He would look at me and grin, then shake his head and tell me not to knock anyone up.

A little while after that, Lucy let me slip my hand under her shirt, then under her bra. Her tits were small, but her nipples would plump to the size of my little finger and just sent shockwaves through me that made me cum even faster. A while later she let me slip my hand into her pants and rub her wet pussy over her panties. Then she let me slip my hand inside her panties and feel her hot, wet pussy without encumbrances. I remembered the exact moment my fingers felt her hot wetness and the little nub of her clit. I could hear her breath in my ear as I lubed up my finger by rubbing it through her folds, then slid it inside her, just a little at first, up to the first knuckle, then the second, then all the way. She grabbed on to me like a kid on a rollercoaster ride and moaned as I fingerfucked the shit out of her until she came. I remembered pulling my hand out of her pussy that first time and holding up to my nose to smell her pungent scent. I licked the juices off my fingers and hummed at the taste. I didn't wash that hand for a month. I would hold my fingers to my nose and jack off with the other hand before going to sleep each night.

Then came the day that Lucy asked me to take out my cock so she could feel it. We were in the back of my dad's old car, parked at a spot near the lake where the kids went to drink and screw. She didn't have to ask me twice. My cock was already hard as a rock and screaming to be set free. I lifted my ass off the seat and shimmied my jeans down my legs as Lucy watched with eyes wide, licking her lips in anticipation. Her fingers tentatively wrapped around my cock, which was long and thick. When she lowered her lips to my cock head and swirled her tongue around the slit, I blew my load all over her face. I was horrified when she looked up with cum dripping off her chin and coating her lips and her hand, even as she continued to slowly work her hand up and down my cock.

"Shit, Lucy, I'm sorry," I muttered.

"Don't be," she said with a smile. She wiped the cum from her chin with two fingers, then stuck the fingers in her mouth and sucked the cum off. She licked her lips and wiggled her eyebrows at me. "Now, it's my turn."

I had no self-control back then. The first time I saw Lucy's pink pussy up close, with the blond curls surrounding her perfect glistening lips, I nearly blew my load again. The first time my fingers spread her lips and my tongue probed deep inside her, I couldn't control my orgasm. I came in my pants again. Lucy smiled and moaned as her juices gushed into my mouth: hot, tangy, salty, wonderful.

Then came the night that Lucy said we could go all the way. I didn't know it, but she had convinced her mom to put her on birth control pills several months before, arguing that it would help ease her terrible menstrual cramps (uh, okay). We had been experimenting for months and had become experts in making each other cum. I knew every inch of Lucy's body and what buttons to push, and she knew mine. Now,

Lucy declared, it was time to put up or shut up. We were going to fuck and that was that. Needless to say, she got no argument from me.

I picked her up in my dad's car and we drove to the lake. We made out for a few minutes with a little hasty foreplay, then the clothes came off and we were ready to do the deed. My cock was like a steel pipe as Lucy's hand stroked up and down the shaft. Her pussy was like a hot well as my fingers slid in and out covered in her juices.

"Lie down," she said as her hand kept milking me. I was a tall kid, thankfully the car was on old Chrysler with a huge back seat, so we had plenty of room. I lay down on the seat with my head against the door and Lucy maneuvered herself on top of me. I held my cock steady as she lowered her pussy onto it. I bit my lip, determined not to cum the second I felt her pussy hole touching the head of my cock. We'd been having sex for months and I had learned to control it a little better, but I'd never slid into a wet pussy before. I held my breath and prayed for control.

"Oh... god..." Lucy moaned as she lowered her hole onto the head of my cock. I was big and we both knew all of me couldn't fit inside her. Being the mathematical genius that she was, I was sure Lucy had made all the calculations in her mind (the average depth of a woman's vagina is 4 to 6 inches, which meant only 40 to 60% of my 10-inch cock would fit inside her). She held onto the back of the seat and slowly let the head of my cock slip inside her. I could feel her young pussy stretching to accommodate my girth, then suctioning tight around the shaft. I thought I was going to cum, but I bit down hard on my lip and tried to focus on my breathing. I put my hands on her hips to help steady her descent. We stared into each other's eyes. I heard her breath out as she lowered herself an inch, then another. Then she gasped when the tip of my cock hit her hymen.

"Let me do it," she whispered. I nodded and kept biting my lip. The feeling of her hot pussy gripping my cock like a thousand tiny fingers was almost more than I could stand. My fingers flexed on her hips. I resisted the urge to just grab her and impale her on my cock.

"Slow..." she moaned, sensing my urgency. I felt her lift off me just a bit, then she let her hips come down quickly. I felt the hymen tear and warmness wash over me. Lucy gasped and froze for a moment as the pain went through her.

"You okay?" I asked.

She swallowed hard and licked her lips. "Yes..." she sighed, eyes closed. "Just let me do it."

Slowly, she started to slide her pussy up and down the length of my shaft, pulling her hips back until the head reached her hole, then sliding back down to take in the first four or five inches. I dug my fingers into her hips and closed my eyes. I had never felt anything so amazing. Her mouth and hands had milked my cock many times before, but that was nothing like the sensation of having her tight pussy suctioning to me. I could feel her hot juices flowing from her pussy, coating the portion of my cock that wouldn't fit inside her. My hands went to her tits and I kneaded her thick nipples between my fingers and I massaged her breasts. It was a pivotal moment of my life. I could still close my eyes today and replay every detail in my mind.

"Oh... god... Calvin..." Lucy moaned and dug her fingers into my chest. "I'm going to cum..." The pain of losing her virginity was gone now, replaced by an intense pleasure that was driving her to increase the motion of her hips. She started hammering her pussy onto me. I could feel the head of my cock hitting her innermost wall. I watched her face, eyes closed, mouth hanging open, twisted in pleasure. "God... Calvin... cum with me..."

Yes! Thank you, Jesus! I grabbed onto her hips and closed my eyes and grunted like a pig as I shot my load into her, filling her with what must have been a gallon of cum. We jerked and twitched and panted and moaned for what seemed like minutes, although the whole thing was probably over in seconds. Afterward, she collapsed in my arms and we lay there sweating all over each other, filling my dad's car with the smell of our sex.

"That was amazing," she said, still struggling to catch her breath. Her fingers tickled my nipple and she gazed up to see if I was smiling. I was, like a happy kid ready to take a nap. "Was that okay for you?"

"That was... unreal," I said, sighing through the words. I pulled her to me and kissed the top of her head. "I love you, Lucy." I didn't think about it. I just said it, because I really did love her and it felt like the right time to say it.

"I love you, too, Calvin," she said as her hand slid down my stomach. Her fingers went around my gooey cock. She gave it a playful tug and smiled when it started to grow in her hand. "And I love what you do to me."

"Good," I said, feeling my young cock getting hard again (there's no such thing as rest between orgasms for teenage boys). "Let's do it again."

# CHAPTER NINE: Lucy

"WOW, WHAT A SMALL WORLD it is," Ed said as he sat behind his desk sipping his coffee like the Mad Hatter. "Who knew my rising star would have history with my new executive producer. I mean, what are the odds?"

"History?" Cole echoed, giving me a sideways smile. "Yes, I guess you could say that we have history. Wouldn't you say, Lucy?"

Ed looked at me with his eyebrows arched in anticipation. I knew what he was thinking. He was hoping that it was good history and not bad history. Cole had told him we were high school sweethearts, but he didn't tell him how things ended between us. I didn't bother telling him that the only thing that tore me and Calvin Walker apart was his dad getting transferred in the middle of our senior year, literally two weeks after we gave each other our virginities. I was devastated that Calvin was moving back to some base in freakin' California. Calvin was devastated, as well, but he was a guy. Emotions came secondary to him. He was sad to be leaving the girl he loved, but he was sadder to be leaving the girl he was now regularly fucking. It was okay. I knew how boys thought. It wasn't that big of a deal. My heart was breaking either way.

We had sex three more times before he moved away. The last time was in my bed on a Saturday afternoon while my folks were at my little brother's softball game. It was the first time we'd ever been in a bed together and I loved the feeling of lying there with his strong arms wrapped around me. And unlike the first time we'd made love where things were done quickly and awkwardly and with a sense of urgency, we made love slowly and passionately, like adults, both knowing that it would be the last time we ever made love, but the one time hopefully we'd both remember forever. I certainly did.

After Calvin moved away, we tried to stay in touch, but it was hard. We emailed and chatted, and called each other when we could. He was an entire country away, and when I was accepted to Stanford and he was accepted to UCLA, the distance between us just seemed to grow. The last conversation we had was short, sweet, and to the point. To his credit, Calvin allowed me to be the one to end it. I love you, but the distance is too great. I need to focus on school now. You need to do the same. We should probably date other people. Okay. Have a good life. Bye.

And that was it. That was the end of our brief, passionate relationship. He moved on and so did I. Seventeen years had passed and now, as fate would have it, I was sitting next to that boy who was now a man. A remarkable looking man, who looked like a magazine ad and smelled like Aramis. And I was now a grown woman who couldn't stop wondering what it would be like to fuck him again after all these years.

"So, Dr. Walker, I was explaining to Lucy before you arrived how well-received your segments are on Friday evenings." Ed leaned forward on his elbows and rubbed his hands together. They made a sound like two blocks of wood rubbing together. "I had not gotten to the part about your contract coming up for renewal."

"Contract renewal?" I frowned at Ed then gave Calvin—Cole— a wary smile. "Uh oh. My first day here and I have to talk to you about your contract renewal?"

"That's being handled by the folks upstairs," Ed said with a look of relief that it wasn't him negotiating directly with Cole. He wouldn't have stood a chance. "And it's my understanding that things are going well. Is that your understanding, Doc?" He looked at Cole with a hopeful smile.

"That's being handled by my manager," Cole said, gracefully deflecting the question. I could tell that he was deflecting by the way his eyebrows arched and his head tipped to the side, like he used to when I'd ask if wanted to stay for dinner on the nights when my mother had made stuffed peppers. He hated stuffed peppers and I knew it. I only asked because I loved to see him sweat. In this case, however, if he was deflecting it was because the negotiations were not going the way Ed thought they were.

"Well, I'm sure things are going well," Ed said, though his voice had lost some of its surety. He leaned back and spread out his hands. "Hopefully, we can expand your role on the program, Doc. And now that I know you and Lucy are old friends, well, I'm sure things will just be lovely."

"Lovely?" I said with a smile. I turned to Cole and nodded at Ed. "I'm pretty sure you're the only person on the planet that would make Ed use that word."

"Lovely is a good word," Cole said, his eyes lingering on mine. He held out his hand and I took it without hesitation. "I can't believe you're here."

"I can't believe it either," I said.

"Um, I hate to break up the reunion, kids," Ed said, still smiling, though I got the impression that the smile was becoming more forced by the minute. He looked at me and tapped the crystal of this watch. "It's almost four. We need to get to the preshow meeting, then we have a show to do."

"I understand," Cole said without letting go of my hand. He turned sideways in the chair and leaned on his elbows to tug me closer. "What time will you be finished tonight?"

"Uh, well," I glanced at Ed because this would be my first newscast and I had no idea what time we'd be done.

"She'll be free by eight," Ed said, the confident smile returning. He didn't have to say it. He loved the fact that his executive producer was an old flame of his rising star. I'm sure in his mind the contract negotiations had just swung in the network's favor. The truth was, he was probably overestimating the influence I had over Dr. Cole Walker after all this time. We were high school sweethearts and hadn't seen each other in nearly twenty years. I seriously doubted anything I had to say would hold sway now.

"Then I will be in a car waiting downstairs at eight," Cole said, squeezing my hand. "Dinner and a game of chess?"

"That sounds *lovely*," I said with a smile. "Though I haven't played chess in years."

"That's okay," he said, getting to his feet and tugging me up with him. He held out his arms and I stepped into them. He whispered in my ear. "Neither have I."

I hadn't done a lot of things in years, I wanted to say, but didn't.

I'd had lots of sex since our last night together, mostly with my shit head ex-husband, but I had never felt the way I had felt in Cole's arms, at least until that moment.

# CHAPTER TEN: Lucy

TO SAY THAT THE REST of my day after Calvin—shit— after Cole left was even more stressful than my morning would have been an understatement. I was used to running the evening news show on a local station in Chicago, a major market, but as Ed kept reminding me, this was the big time. The big leagues. The big show. I think those were all baseball references meaning that I was now playing with the big boys. Regardless of the reference, I understood what he meant. I was now executive producing a network newscast that would be seen by millions of viewers around the globe five nights a week in prime time, which meant that if something went wrong, millions would see it and I would be to blame. Then some asshole would post the video on YouTube and I would be a viral sensation and a laughing stock of the industry. I tried to ignore the intense pressure of the situation and the nagging self-doubt and I told myself that I had earned this spot because I was good at my job. Still, I kept my fingers laced together behind my back for most of the afternoon so no one would see my hands shaking.

Ed stayed with me the entire time as I met with the team two hours ahead of air to map out that evening's broadcast and arrange the lineup, then stood next to me in the control booth as I barked out orders to the team in the booth and on the studio floor. If I pressed a button on the console in front of me I could speak directly into the ears of the anchors on set. Each time I'd say something in Bryant's earpiece, he'd stare into the camera and give me a stony look. Stephanie smiled and gave a slight nod when I gave her directions, though I think it was mostly because she was amused that just the sound of my voice seemed to irritate the shit out of Bryant. It was controlled chaos and there were a couple of minor glitches, but all in all, it wasn't a terrible first night on the job.

"Well, congratulations, Lucy. Your network cherry is officially popped," Ed said with a sigh of relief as the ending credits rolled. Everyone in the booth stood to give me a polite round of applause. The monitors showing the set went dark as Bryant and Stephanie walked off to their respective dressing rooms and the camera operators switched the cameras off. I took out my earpiece and set it on the control panel.

"I feel like I've been popped," I said with a sigh of relief that matched his. I gave him a sideways look and wiggled my eyebrows. "That was fucking amazing."

"It's an adrenaline rush," Ed said. He patted my shoulder. "You did great. Just the right amount of bossiness and tact. Hell, I think I even saw Bryant smile at one point."

"I seriously doubt that," I said, shaking my head. "But I'll win him over."

"I know you will," Ed said. He held open the control room door to let me pass, then led the way back toward his office. "Do you think you can win over Dr. Cole Walker?"

I stopped and turned to face him. "What do you mean?"

He hitched his pants up beneath his round stomach, then rubbed his eyes and blew out a long breath. He suddenly looked very tired. "Honestly, I don't think the contract negotiations with Walker are going in our favor, Lucy."

"What makes you say that?"

"I got a call from upstairs while you were doing the news," Ed said, slowly shaking his head. "Walker's agent delivered new terms this afternoon after we met with the good doctor. We want to renew him at double the current rate with the same amount of time onset. He wants to quadruple the rate, double the minutes, and a guarantee of a thirty-minute special once a quarter on the medical topic of his choice. And he wants an anytime-opt-out clause, which is fucking unheard of in this business."

I folded my arms over my chest and leaned back against the wall to give others room to pass by. Ed leaned his shoulder against the wall and shoved his hands into his pockets. He was so round he couldn't help but block the hallway. I asked, "Why does he want an anytime-opt-out?"

Ed blew out another long breath that puffed up his cheeks like blowfish. "Word is he's negotiating with Kingston Television about a daily syndicated show."

"A daily show? Seriously?"

"Yep. He wants to be the next Dr. Oz."

"Wow, that's..."

"Awful," Ed growled. "If he gets a syndication deal, the opt-out clause would let him pull out of our deal anytime he wanted with no notice or penalty."

"Would that be so bad?" I asked. "I mean, he's only on once a week for two minutes."

"Those two minutes are the highest rated minutes of the week for us," Ed said, holding up two fingers and stabbing the air with them. "Sure, we can put another talking head in his place. I've got them lined up around the fucking block. But they are not Dr. Cole Walker. Him leaving could cost us millions in lost revenue and tons of lost viewers who will follow him wherever he goes."

I tried not to smile. Who knew that one day my old high school sweetheart who got nervous raising his hand in class would command such an audience. The look on Ed's face told me there would be absolutely nothing to smile about if Cole left the show. I shouldn't have asked, but I did. "Okay, so, what can I do help?"

Ed looked at me for a few seconds, then his bushy eyebrows slowly rose and he twisted his mouth to the side. "I think you know. Give him a reason to stay."

I huffed at him. "You can't be serious." My face turned deep red, not because of what he'd said, but because I had been thinking about fucking Cole since the moment I saw him walk through the door. However, I was not so egotistical as to think that my pussy still held any type of control over his brain or cock. I'd done a quick Google of Dr. Cole Walker after our meeting. He was a notorious womanizer and had his pick of models, actresses, and heiresses. There was no room for someone like me in his life. I was an old flame and nothing more.

"I'm not telling you to do anything you're not already thinking about doing," Ed said nonchalantly with one round shoulder going up and down. "I'm just suggesting that maybe you could get him to see our side of things."

"You want me to negotiate his contract on my back." I rolled my eyes at him. "I don't think I have that kind of influence on him anymore."

"Don't kid yourself," Ed said, pushing away from the wall. He leaned in and lowered his voice. "I saw the way he looked at you. I think you have far more influence than you know."

He glanced at his watch. It was almost eight o'clock.

"I gotta get home. And you gotta get downstairs." He put his hand on my arm and squeezed. There was a devilish grin on his pudgy face. "Prince Charming awaits."

# CHAPTER ELEVEN: Cole

I'M NOT GOING TO LIE. I was a little nervous when I saw Lucy come out of the building and head my way. It was an odd feeling. I had not been nervous around a woman in... well... years. I was a cocky son of a bitch and damn proud of it. I made people nervous, not the other way around. Don't judge me. It was hard not to have an ego the size of Texas when you did what I did for a living, literally holding life and death in your hands one minute, then holding the attention of millions of fans worldwide the next. My fans hung on my every word, post, and Tweet. It was the damnedest thing you ever saw. Being me was almost like being a movie star or a rock star. All modesty aside, when you looked like I looked and did what I did and screwed the women I screwed, well, again, it was hard not to let it go to your head.

The oddest thing was that I didn't feel the need to show off around Lucy. I had not seen this woman in nearly twenty years and the moment I saw her I felt my entire body relax, as if every muscle sighed at the sight of her. She moved into my arms and melted to me as if we had never been apart. I was totally comfortable around her. There was no pretense. No bullshit. I was completely at ease. It would be interesting to see if that kept up during dinner or if my famous ego would rear its ugly head. The Lucy I used to know would cut me off at the knees if I got too cocky with her. I'd have to keep that in mind as the evening progressed.

"How was your first broadcast?" I asked as she approached with a big smile on her face. "I saw some of it in the car. It looked perfect to me."

"It went great, but I need a drink," she said, giving me a hug before climbing into the back of the limo. I climbed in behind her and closed the door. I took a deep breath. The faint scent of her soap and shampoo lingered in my nostrils, making me sigh. The driver glanced over his shoulder to make sure we were in, then pulled slowly away from the curb while we got settled in the back.

"What would you like?" I asked, gesturing at the minibar built into the back of the front seat. I gave her a playful frown. "Wait a minute, when did you start drinking?"

"Uh, when I turned twenty-one," she said with a smile that was as contagious as the flu. "In fact, I had my very first hangover the morning after my twenty-first birthday. I'll just take a beer if you have it. What about you? When did you start developing your bad habits?"

I smiled. The fact that I'd never tasted a drop of alcohol was one of those pompous things I liked to brag about. "I've developed many bad habits over the years, but alcohol isn't one of them," I said as I opened the mini fridge beneath the bar and plucked out a bottle of Coors Lite and twisted off the cap for her. I wrapped the bottle in a napkin and handed it to her.

"You don't drink?" She said it as if she were astounded by the fact. She settled back in the seat and took a sip of the beer and let out a sigh. "Good for you. What about drugs?"

"Oh, there you got me. I am a crack addict of the highest magnitude," I said making a silly face. I took a bottle of Perrier from the fridge and sat sideways in the seat facing her. "Actually, I've never taken a drug, never smoked a joint, never been drunk or high. I overdosed on sinus meds once in college, but that's the depth of my drug addiction."

"Are you philosophically opposed to alcohol and drugs?" she asked. I watched her tongue circle around her lips after taking a drink. "Or do you just think it's cool to be different?"

"I wouldn't say that I'm philosophically opposed," I said, holding out the Perrier bottle to tap it to hers. "When I was younger, I was too busy trying to keep my grades up to get into med school to get drunk or high. I was always the designated driver or the one sober frat brother who dealt with the cops when they came to bust up a party. Now, I'm always on call, so I have to make sure I'm always sober and ready to go."

"My goodness, look at you, all grown up," she said, smiling at me. "Little Calvin Walker, a world-class cardiologist and TV star. I always knew you had talented hands, Calvin, but I would never have imagined this. How cool is it being you?"

"It's very cool," I said, wiggling my fingers at her, making her giggle. "But I'm sure Ed told you everything there is to know about me. Let's talk about you."

"You're much more interesting," she said with a sigh.

"I'm only as interesting as other people think I am," I said, rolling my eyes. "Come on, Lucinda Walsh Rhodes, catch me up on your life over the last eighteen years." I held out my hands and she took a deep breath, then told me her life story, at least the highlights and lowlights, of the past eighteen years.

She went to Stanford after high school, met her future husband her sophomore year, fell in love even though everyone warned her that he was a pussy-chasing douchebag (her words), graduated with a degree in journalism, moved back to Milwaukee, got a job as an assistant news producer at the local CBS affiliate, moved to Chicago to become an executive producer at the CBS affiliate there, caught her husband cheating multiple times, finally had enough, left him and...

"Here I am," she said quietly, as if telling the story had exhausted her. She had peeled the label off the beer bottle with her thumbnail as she spoke. She brushed the scraps of paper into her palm and dropped them on the minibar. There was a sad tinge to her voice now, as if she wasn't really where she expected to be at this point in her life.

"And here you are," I said. "Where did you think you would be at this point in your life?"

Her pretty nose crinkled when she frowned at me. "I'm not sure what you mean."

"You said, here I am," I said, my hand sliding through the air like some game show model presenting a prize. "Is this where you thought you would be when you were that bright-eyed journalism student at Stanford? Did you think that one day you'd be the executive producer of a cable news broadcast? I mean, you must be pretty proud of where you are, Lucy, all things considered."

"All things considered I suppose I am," she said, mustering a smile that could have construed as happy or sad.

"Well, however things were supposed to work out," I said, taking her hand and giving it a squeeze. "I, for one, am glad you are right here, right now."

"Me, too," she said, her eyes beginning to sparkle again. "I can't think of anywhere else I'd rather be."

"Good, me too," I said. I brought her hand to my lips and gave it a playful kiss. "So, dinner? What sounds good?"

Lucy's fingers tightened around mine and she leaned toward me. She pressed her lips softly to mine and slipped her tongue into my mouth. Pulling back, she rubbed her nose against mine and said, "What I'm hungry for they don't serve in restaurants. Take me to your place, Calvin. And hurry, before I change my mind."

# CHAPTER TWELVE: Lucy

I HEARD MYSELF SAYING the words, but for a moment, I wasn't sure if I'd said them out loud or just inside my head. The tip of my nose was touching his. Our eyes were locked just inches apart. Our hot breath mingled like steam rising through a fog. Cole smiled. I smiled. His fingers tightened around my hand. Obviously, he'd heard the words I'd blurted without thinking. Thank goodness, because I didn't think I had the nerve to say them again.

COLE ORDERED THE DRIVER to take us to his penthouse, then raised the tinted glass behind the front seat so we could have a little privacy. We sat in the back seat making out like the two horny teenagers we once were.

His tongue hungrily probed my mouth as his warm hand slipped under my blouse and bra to massage my breast and roll my nipples. Little sparks of electricity shot through my body from head to toe, as if I'd touched an electric fence.

I could feel the intense flood gushing between my legs as my hand slid between his thighs and found his thick cock hard and ready, just like the old days. It felt magical beneath my hand, as if touching it had transported me back in time.

I moaned into his mouth when his hand slid down to my crotch. He rubbed the fabric between my legs until the heat was so intense I thought my slacks might catch fire.

"We're here," he sighed in my ear as the car rolled to a stop in front of his Manhattan penthouse. It was a short ride that ended not a moment too soon. "Let's continue this upstairs."

"Yes, let's," I said, blowing out a long breath and adjusting my blouse as the doorman hurried across the sidewalk to open the car door.

"I have a huge boner," Cole whispered with a boyish grin that I recognized from years ago. He took off his jacket to drape over his arm to cover his protruding cock. He slid out of the car and held out his free hand to me.

When I got out of the car I "accidentally" brushed his cock with my hand. He jumped and I giggled.

"Let's go upstairs and I'll take care of that for you, Dr. Walker," I said. Without another word, he grabbed my hand and literally dragged me inside the building, across the marble foyer, into the gold-paneled elevator, and into his penthouse suite.

We attacked each other the moment the elevator doors closed.

COLE LED ME THROUGH the dark penthouse, not bothering to turn on lights until we reached his bedroom, which was larger than my entire apartment. One wall was all glass with a magnificent view of the city at night. A king-sized bed was centered on the opposite wall. Cole sat on the edge of the bed and held my hands.

"I've missed you, Lucy," he said, his eyes soft in the glow of the bedside lamp. "I've dreamt of you over the years."

"You have?" I asked, twirling my hands through his thick black hair. "And what did you dream?"

He put his hands on my hips and pulled me toward him. As his fingers worked the buttons on the front of my blouse, he gazed up and spoke softly. "I've dreamt of fucking you. I've dreamt about eating your pussy. About your lips on my cock. About my cock deep inside you."

"Mmmm, I like the way you dream," I said as he pushed my blouse off my shoulders. The bra I was wearing hooked in the front. He had it open quickly and my bra joined the blouse on the floor. My big tits bounced free.

"God, when did you get these?" he asked with a devilish grin as he massaged my round globes.

"The year you left me behind," I said. "Now, aren't you sad that you went away?"

"I'll just have to make up for lost time," he said. My areolas were large and dark, my nipples the size of pink thimbles. He squeezed them between his fingers. "I remember your nipples being long and wonderfully suckable."

"They still are," I said, my breathing growing heavy from his touch. "See for yourself."

"Don't mind if I do." He cupped my tits and swirled his tongue around my nipples. My tits were large enough that he could squeeze them together and slide his tongue between my nipples without leaving my breast. I twirled his hair around my fingers and closed my eyes as he suckled me. I could feel the hot juices pooling between my pussy lips, soaking my panties. The scent of my tangy juices filled the air.

Cole unbuttoned my slacks and hooked his thumbs in the sides, then pushed my slacks and panties down my legs at the same time. He glanced at my shaved cunt and smiled. "I love that," he said as his thumbs pulled back the skin above my clit, making me jump. "I remember this being covered in blonde curls."

"I can grow it back," I said playfully. My voice was husky, breathless. When he pressed his thumbs against the sides of my clit and moved them around, I could feel myself about to cum. When he slid his fingers down through my folds, lubricating them with my hot juices, then slid two fingers inside me, I didn't bother holding back. I clutched his head between my tits and let the orgasm come.

"Fuck... Cole... I'm cumming...."

"Cum my darling," he said, his teeth on my nipple, his fingers jackhammering into my cunt. His free hand went around me and clutched my ass cheeks to lift me to my toes. "Soak my hand with your hot pussy juices."

I smiled at the dirty talk. The only dirty talk I'd ever participated in was when Randy and I would pass each other in the hallway and I'd tell him to go fuck himself. The teenage me would have been embarrassed by the talk. And the teenage Cole never said a word when we were doing it. I'd never been with a dirty talker before. I found it totally fucking hot.

"Oh... my god... yessss..." I came in a great wave that coated his entire hand with my juices. When the orgasm finally ceased, I opened my eyes to see him licking his fingers.

"You taste... lovely," he said with a sly grin. "Now, it's my turn."

He directed me to sit on the bed and he stood in front of me. My heart was still racing as my trembling fingers started unbuttoning his shirt. He tore open the bottom two buttons and tugged the shirt off his arms and tossed it aside. My mouth practically dropped when I looked at his muscular body. Cole was no longer a skinny kid with no chest hair or muscle tone. His body looked like it had been freakin' Photoshopped. His shoulders and chest were thick with heavy muscle. Veins roped his biceps and forearms. His rippling abs moved slowly in and out as he breathed. His chest was covered with black curls that encircled his dark nipples.

"Wow," I said, my hands going over his chest. His nipples were like hard pebbles under my fingers. I smiled up at him. "You really filled out."

"You ain't seen nothing yet," he said, putting his hands on this sides like he was Superman. He nodded at the huge bulge protruding from the front of his pants. "Keep going."

My fingers fumbled with the belt buckle and zipper for a moment, trembling in anticipation as my palms brushed the head of his cock. I pushed the pants down his leg and smiled at his cock pushing against the black satin briefs he wore. I hooked my fingers in the front of the waistband and pulled his underwear out and down to free his long cock. When I saw his cock spring up, I literally felt myself starting to cum again.

"Oh, my," I said, licking my lips. "You've filled out all over."

When we were kids, Cole's cock was long and thick, but time and age seemed to have filled it out even more. His cock was at least ten inches long and as round as the mouth of a shot glass. The shaft was arrow straight and veiny. His cock head was the size of a small plum, dark purple, ready to pop. His pubes were thick and black, like the hair on his head.

I wrapped my fingers around his cock and started slowly milking him back and forth. "Tell me what you want me to do," I said, glancing up with a coy smile. "Tell me what you want me to do with your big, thick cock."

He put his hands on my shoulders and breathed through his open lips as he gazed down at me. "I want you to suck my big cock," he growled. "I want you to lick the juices from the slit and pump it hard with your hand while you suck on the head."

"You want me to play with your balls while I suck your big cock?" I asked. I leaned forward and rubbed the tip of his cock against my nipples, leaving little juice trails along the way. I slid my other hand under him to massage his balls and gently rub his taint. "What else do you want me to do to you?"

"I want you to take my cock down your throat," he said, spreading his legs so my finger could rub little circles around his asshole. He put his hands on my head and pulled me toward him. "Suck my cock, Lucy. Suck it now."

I held his cock steady and pressed my wet lips to the tip. I squeezed the shaft from the base to the head. Tiny drops of juice oozed from the slit. I licked them away like melting ice cream on a hot summer's day. I spread my lips just enough to let the bulbous head slide into my mouth. My tongue swirled around the underside of the head in the spot where the nerves all came together. Cole moaned and pulled me closer.

I suctioned my lips around the shaft and let an inch slide in. I sucked as I pulled my lips back, then slid two inches inside my mouth. I pulled back again, then slid in three, then four. When the head of his cock hit the back of my throat, a full six inches inside my mouth, I slid my lips back over his shaft, then drove him in again.

"Fucking hell, that feels amazing," Cole sighed. I worked my finger into his tight asshole as I sucked his cock. He squirmed at the pain, but didn't ask me to stop. I took my lips from his wet cock and started pumping him with my hand while my finger slid and out of his ass. I watched him enjoy the ride. His eyes were closed. Every muscle in his beautiful body was tense. His mouth was hanging open. He was panting like a dog.

"I want you to fuck me, Cole," I said, my hands slowing the pace so he wouldn't shoot his load before I had him inside me. He opened his eyes and smiled.

"Tell me what you want," he said. "Talk dirty to me, Lucy."

"I want your big cock inside my tight pussy," I said. I had no idea where this nasty talk was coming from but damned if it wasn't a turn on. "I want you to hammer my pussy until I scream. I want you to squeeze my nipples and squeeze my ass. I want you to do everything you've ever dreamed of doing to me."

He smiled. "That may take a while."

I let go of his cock and pushed back on the bed with my legs spread wide. "Then you'd better get to it."

# CHAPTER THIRTEEN: Cole

HOLY FUCKING SHIT. I've had some great blowjobs in my day, but the way Lucy was sucking my cock and reaming my ass was just about to put me over the motherfucking moon. I could hold back my orgasm until I was ready to pop, but I knew that a couple more minutes of that action was going to make it impossible to hold back. And the dirty talk! I fucking loved that fucking shit. Some women are put off by it. Fuck, Lucy was giving back as good as she was getting.

She pushed herself back onto the bed and spread her legs to give me a perfect view of her bare pussy. The lips were perfect and pink, glistening with her juices. She used two fingers to pull back the skin from her clit to show me the little man in the boat. I wanted to fuck the shit out of her, but I couldn't resist having a little taste of her pussy first.

I got to my knees and slid my hands under her ass and cupped her cheeks and lifted her off the bed. I was gonna eat her like a fucking ear of corn! I flicked my tongue over her clit and she jerked and moaned. "Mmmm, you taste wonderful," I said as my tongue slid between her folds, tasting her hot, tangy juices for the first time in years. She tasted as sweet and salty as I remembered. She slid her fingers down to spread her pussy lips for me. I flattened my tongue and lapped her up, licking from her asshole to her clit and back again, like a hungry kitten lapping up milk. I stiffened my tongue like a little cock and slid it deep inside her, then bobbed my head back and forth to fuck her with it. She bucked her ass against my face, covering my cheeks and chin with her hot juices.

"Fuck me..." she moaned, her fingers in my hair. "Calvin... Cole... I want your big cock inside me... now..."

I wiped my mouth on my shoulder and climbed between her legs. She reached between us and took my cock in her hand and guided me toward her pulsating pussy.

"Fuck... you feel amazing..." she moaned as the head of my cock slid inside her tight hole. Her legs went around my waist and she pressed her heels to my ass to prod me on. "Fuck me... fuck me with your big cock..."

I smiled and did as I was told. I braced my arms on the bed and slowly let my cock slide inside her until I felt the head press against the back of her cunt. I pulled all the way out and slid all the way in again. With each thrust, the tempo grew faster, until I was ramming into her so hard the entire bed shook. She dug her fingernails into my arms and moaned my name.

I watched her face as the orgasm drew near. She was beautiful, even more beautiful than the day I met her in math class all those years ago. Even more beautiful than the night she climbed on top of my cock for the first time in the back of my dad's car. She was fully a woman now, with large breasts and a tight, shaved pussy and lips that took me back in time.

"Oh... fuck... I'm cumming..." she said, rocking her hips up to meet my cock as it rammed deep inside her. "Cum with me... Cole... Cum... Fill my pussy with your hot load..."

I let go of the breath that I'd been holding and let myself cum. I could feel my balls tightening as the cum erupted from my cock like a volcano. "Fuck... yes... god... your pussy is so fucking tight... I'm cumming, Lucy... oh... fuck yes... I'm cumming..."

Our bodies jerked and spasmed together as we came at the exact same time. I could feel her hot juices gushing out over me, drenching the part of my shaft that wouldn't fit inside her and my balls and my pubes. I stiffened as I shot my load deep inside her, filling her with my hot milky cum. A few more thrusts and she wrapped her arms around my neck and pulled me down on the bed beside her. We were both covered in sweat and panting like we'd just run a marathon and fucked at the finish line.

"Holy shit, that was amazing," she said, putting a hand over her left breast. "My heart is about to pound right out of my chest."

"It was a little like going back in time," I said, turning my head so I could see her face.

"It was better," she said, smiling back at me. "Because this time we knew what the heck we were doing."

LUCY SAT ACROSS THE breakfast table wearing nothing but one of my white dress shirts and a smile. What was it that was so fucking sexy about a woman wearing a man's dress shirt? Whatever it was it made me want to rip the shirt off her and take her right there on the table. Or maybe I'd just pick up the bottle of maple syrup and pour it over her big tits and lick it off. I glanced at my watch. I had a consult in thirty minutes. Breakfast sex would have to wait. I picked up my coffee cup and watched her finish off the entire stack of pancakes I'd made for both of our breakfasts.

"How many pancake eating contests have you won over the last twenty years?" I asked, arching my eyebrows in wonder.

"Every single one I entered, smart ass," she said, dropping her fork onto her empty plate and licking the syrup from her lips. "When did you learn to cook?"

"I don't think making pancakes technically qualifies as cooking," I said. "Anything you can make from a recipe on the side of a box of powder isn't really cooking."

"Call it what you will, that was freakin' delicious," she said with a contented smile. "I can't believe I'm here with you like this. It's a little weird, huh."

"Just a little," I said, smiling back. "I'm glad you're here, though. In fact, I would really like for you to be here a lot more. We have a lot of catching up to do, in more ways than one."

"I don't want to cramp your style, Dr. Walker," she said, holding out her hands. "I mean, you have been voted one of New York's Most Eligible Bachelors five years in a row. I don't want the press to get the wrong impression here."

I rolled my eyes and snorted at her. "You really have to stay off Google," I said. "I'm not asking you to marry me. I'm just saying that I'd love to see more of you. You make me happy, Lucy. It's a nice feeling."

"Have you not been happy, Calvin?" she asked, a look of concern washing over her face. "I mean, Cole?"

"Oh, I've been happy," I said with a halfhearted shrug. "It's just nice having an old friend back in my life."

"An old friend?" She gave me a pouty look. "Is that what I am to you? An old friend? Like an old frat buddy?"

"More of an old flame then," I said, the smile melting into a sigh. "One that I would very much like to kindle to see what ignites."

"I think that can be arranged," she said. She pulled her knees up and wrapped her arms around them. "Can I ask you a serious question?"

"You can ask me anything," I said. I drained the coffee cup and got up to put it and the breakfast dishes in the sink. I turned to lean back against the counter with my arms folded over my chest. "Shoot."

"Are you thinking about leaving WNN?"

"Is that something we should be discussing?" I asked, a little put off by the question.

She rested her chin on her knees to gaze up at me. "Is there a reason why we shouldn't discuss it?"

"No, not unless last night was just a ploy by the network to get me to renew the current contract on their terms. Please tell me you weren't sent here by Ed Quigley to ply me with sexual favors."

She rolled her eyes. "Of course not. Unless you think that would work."

I chuckled and shook my head. "My career is in the hands of my agent and manager now, Lucy. I'll do whatever they think is best for the long term. Right now, that would be to renew with WNN under more favorable terms, however..."

"However, there's the syndication deal with Kingston Television," she said.

"You know about that?"

"Everybody knows about that," she said, swatting a hand at me. "Ed said you want an opt-out clause in case the syndication deal happened down the road. Do you think that's going to happen, Cole? Are you going to be the next Dr. Oz?"

I narrowed my eyes at her and took a deep breath. I wasn't used to anyone questioning my reasoning or prying into my business, but this was Lucy, the girl I had once loved madly and could easily do so again. I looked at my watch and pushed away from the counter.

"I really have to go, Lucy," I said. "We can talk about this another time."

"Just make me a promise," she said, getting up from the table and wrapping her arms around my neck. The shirt rose off her ass and I couldn't resist helping myself to a handful or two. "If you do decide to leave, just give me a little notice. I mean, I'm the executive producer now, it's technically my show, and it would be nice to avoid a major catastrophe my first week on the job." She rubbed her nose to my chin. "Besides, you know I hate surprises as much as you do."

"I don't know about that," I said, kissing the tip of her nose. "This surprise seems to be working out nicely."

# CHAPTER FOURTEEN: Lucy

THE NEXT TWO WEEKS were a blur of activity, both at work and at home, where most nights found me wrapped in Cole's strong arms. The sex was constant, hot, intense, primal, like two wild animals that couldn't wait to tear into each other's bodies the moment they were alone. I woke up some mornings so tired and sore I could barely walk, but by bedtime, I was right back in the game and ready for more. Some nights we spent hours exploring each other's bodies like sexual forensic detectives. Other nights, our lovemaking was soft and tender and deeply passionate and over quickly because we no longer had anything to prove. Regardless of the ferocity of the sex, when it was over, Cole would lift his muscled arm and I would snuggle into his side with my head resting on his chest and fall fast asleep. We reconnected and caught up quickly. Even though our lives could not have been more different, it really was like we had never been apart.

Work was never slow or easy. To the contrary, producing a one-hour live network newscast was like juggling a dozen running chainsaws in the air while tap dancing on hot coals and whistling Dixie out of your ass. It was fast-paced, frenetic, chaotic, and absolutely wonderful. A total adrenaline rush night after night. After two weeks on the job, even Bryant gave me an occasional smile at the end of the newscast. I considered that a big step in getting the famously cranky anchor on my side.

It was weird when Cole came on set every Friday to do his two-minute segment. We didn't try to hide the fact that we were sleeping together, but we didn't advertise it either. Just to make sure there was no conflict of interest, and to keep the rumor mill running at a minimum when Cole came onset, I stayed in the control booth and resisted the urge to whisper filthy things in his earpiece. Cole would slide into the chair beside Stephanie at the news desk while an assistant clipped on his wireless microphone. He would make small talk with Stephanie and Bryant before the cameras came on. It was apparent how enamored they both were of him. Even Bryant couldn't seem to stop smiling at him. And who wouldn't be in awe of Dr. Cole Walker? He looked like a Greek god sitting next to an aging Ken and bouncing Barbie. Stephanie giggled like a horny teenager at his every word and constantly put her hand on his. Cole would casually pull his hand away and smile at the camera, knowing that I was watching.

I was sure the only person who knew I was seeing Cole was Ed, and even he hadn't mentioned anything about it until the Friday afternoon that he came into my office with a grim look on his face an hour before show time. He closed the door and slumped in the chair across from my desk.

"What's wrong, Ed?" I asked, alarmed by the deep frown cutting across his forehead. Ed's usual expression was a frown, but this was different. "Did somebody die?"

"Yes, our Friday ratings," he said with a heavy sigh. "I just got off the phone with the guys upstairs. Dr. Cole Walker is not renewing his contract because he got an offer to do a syndicated show for Kingston Television. He will not be here today for his usual Friday spot or in the future, so we'll need to fill the time with something else until we can line up a replacement talking head. His time at WNN is through."

I blinked at him because I couldn't believe what I was hearing. Cole and I had not discussed his contract negotiations with WNN since the morning after we reconnected two weeks ago, and he hadn't mentioned a word about the syndication deal coming to fruition. Surely, he would have shared such monumental news with me. I mean, we weren't officially a couple or anything, but Jesus, when you spend most nights with a guy's cock inside you, you expect a little consideration.

I picked up my phone to see if I had missed a message from Cole. I hadn't. The last time I'd talked to him was at breakfast around seven. I knew that he had a heart valve replacement surgery scheduled for mid-morning, so I just assumed he was really busy. I set the phone aside and stared back at Ed.

I asked, "When did this happen?"

"I just got the call five minutes ago that the deal is officially dead," he said with a shrug. "But it's my understanding that Walker's manager gave our people notice yesterday. They tried to hammer out a last-minute deal, but it was too late. Walker signed with Kingston Television yesterday and there will be a press release today. Turns out, we were probably just a bargaining chip he was using to get a better deal in syndication, the son of a bitch."

"Yesterday? You're fucking kidding me. He signed the deal yesterday?" I felt the heat rising from my chest into my head, like lava flowing up to the top of a volcano about to blow sky high. "That son of a bitch."

Ed cocked his head at me and frowned. "What?"

"He didn't say anything to me about the deal," I said, nostrils flaring like an angry bull. "And he didn't say that he wouldn't be here for the show today, either."

Ed narrowed his eyes at me. "Have you two talked about his plans?" he asked, trying to act nonchalant but failing miserably. "Are you sure you didn't know this was coming?"

I blinked at him. "What? No, of course not. I mean, we briefly talked about it when I first got into town, but he made it clear it was not something he wanted to discuss with me." It was my turn to frown back at him. "Why would you ask me that?"

Ed took a deep breath and blew it out slowly. He put his elbows on his knees and leaned over them, then spread his hands. "I won't sugarcoat it for you, Lucy. Management is concerned that there may have been a conflict of interest at play. They know you and Walker were seeing each other and there is speculation that maybe Walker or his people used that relationship to his advantage."

My blood ran cold as I stared into his eyes. "That's ridiculous," I said, gritting my teeth, doing my best to retain my composure. "We never discussed it. And I certainly would not have revealed anything about WNN's position. Fuck, Ed, I didn't know anything to reveal!"

"I know that," Ed said with a heavy sigh. "I told them that, but they have egg all over their faces and they're looking for someone to blame. They think you knew about Walker's plans and just didn't say anything."

"They think I picked my lover over my job."

"Pretty much, yeah."

I leaned back with my arms folded defensively over my chest. "Ed, how did management know that Cole and I were seeing each other? The only people here who knew that for sure were you and me. Did you tell them about us?"

Rather than get defensive and try to deny the truth, Ed pushed himself back in the chair and gave me a slow nod. "Yeah, Lucy, I'm afraid I did. I was having lunch with Larry David in programming and let it slip that you two were high school sweethearts and there might be a rekindling of the flame. Honestly, it was just a quick comment made in passing. I never suspected it would come back to bite you in the ass."

I felt the muscles in my jaws tighten. "Is this going to bite me in the ass, Ed? Is my job in jeopardy?"

His round shoulders went up and down. "Honestly, Lucy, I don't know. Management would like to meet with both of us on Monday to discuss the situation."

"Fuck..." I slumped back in the chair and rubbed my eyes. "Oh well, it was fun while it lasted."

"There's something else, Lucy," Ed said. "I just mentioned to Larry that you two were old flames. That was at lunch over a week ago.

However, when I talked to Larry today he seemed to know every detail of the relationship. Or at least acted like he did."

"What do you mean?"

Ed glanced over his shoulder at the door to make sure it was closed. He leaned forward and lowered his voice. "He asked me how a woman could fuck a man every night for two weeks and not know what was on his mind."

My mouth dropped open. It was such a ludicrous question that I had to smile. "What?"

"You heard it right. Those were his exact words. My question to you is, how does Larry David in programming know that you've spent every night for two weeks fucking Dr. Cole Walker?"

"How indeed?"

We stared at each other for a moment, both knowing the answer, then Ed put his palms on his knees to push himself out of the chair. "We'll get it all cleared up on Monday, Lucy. Don't let it ruin your weekend."

"I'm afraid it's too late for that," I said, looking up with a forced smile that was anything but happy.

Ed nodded. "I know. And I'm sorry. What are you going to do?"

"I have a show to produce," I said, glancing at my watch. "Then? Who the fuck knows?"

# CHAPTER FIFTEEN: Cole

FIFTEEN MILLION DOLLARS.

Fifteen *fucking* million dollars.

That's how much Kingston Television was going to pay me under the three-year syndication deal I had signed yesterday. They would also put up the money to produce five, one-hour shows per week and get the show syndicated into every market in the country by the end of the year. There were also six-figure bonuses for meeting ratings milestones every quarter and the promise of more good things to come if the show caught on like they believed it would.

One of the best parts was that I could recruit and hire my own staff. In my mind, there was no one better to executive produce the show than the woman who was walking into my kitchen at that very moment. I pulled a bottle of Coors from the fridge and twisted off the top and set it on the kitchen island. I knew better than to offer her a glass. Lucy liked her beer ice cold straight out of the bottle. I gave her time to drop her computer bag in a chair and was about to give her the great news when she pounced on me with her teeth and claws extended.

"I can't fucking believe you did this to me," she said, balling her hands into tight fists and shaking them in the air between us. "I thought you cared about me, Cole. How could you keep this from me?"

I planted my palms on the island and gave her a confused look. "Excuse me?"

"The syndication deal," she said, throwing her hands in the air as if she were tossing pizza dough. "Why didn't you fucking tell me you had signed a deal?"

"Actually, I was about to," I said, sounding less irritated than I really felt. My good mood darkened quickly. I was not accustomed to this kind of assault and would normally strike back in force. Even though it was Lucy, I didn't appreciate her tone and without thinking, went on the defensive. "What's your problem?"

"My fucking problem is that I find out an hour before air time that you are bailing on my show!"

"Bailing on *your* show? Seriously?" I shook my head at her. "Lucy, you've been the executive producer for two weeks. You can hardly call it your show. And I'm not bailing on anyone, most of all you."

"It is my fucking show and you are bailing," she said, her face turning a decidedly unattractive shade of red. "You promised that you would give me a heads up if you were not going to renew your deal with WNN."

"Actually, I didn't promise you any sort of thing," I said. "You asked me to, but I never said I would give you a heads up about anything. I told you, that was all in the hands of my manager and agent. It wasn't something I would discuss with you."

"You fucking asshole," she said, spitting the words. She put her hands to her head in dramatic style and gawked at me. "You used me."

That one made my head spin. I shook my head and frowned at her. "What? How did I use you?"

"I told you how bad Ed wanted you to renew the contract. How bad I wanted you to. I'm sure you told your agent that you were fucking the show's new executive producer. Your agent used that knowledge to work the deal with Kingston. He told them they needed to sign you before I could convince you to stay at WNN."

"Give me a break, Lucy," I said with an exasperated sigh. "I already knew how badly WNN wanted to renew my contract. Christ, they've offered to do everything short of having Stephanie Hart suck my cock on the air to make it happen."

"That would have certainly gotten you ratings and your rocks off," she said angrily. "I'm sure Bryant would have fondled your balls while Stephanie blew you!" She folded her arms over her chest and glared at me. "Be honest with me, Calvin. Why didn't you tell me?"

I took a deep breath and threw up my hands. "Fine, my agent told me not to, okay? He was afraid you'd say something to Ed and fuck up the deal."

"You didn't think that you could trust me?" Her tone went soft and her eyes filled up with tears. "Oh my god, that's it, isn't it? You didn't trust me enough to tell me the truth. You were afraid I'd fuck up your deal."

"I was getting ready to tell you that now," I said. "I was going to give you the news and carry out on the town to celebrate."

She covered her eyes with her hands and shook her head. For the love of freakin' god, why did women have to be so goddamn hysterical?

"You don't trust me," she said again as she picked up her computer bag and slung the strap over her shoulder. "And now you've probably cost me my job."

"What are you talking about?" I came around the bar and tried to put my hand on her shoulder, but she jerked away. "Lucy, what are you talking about?"

"Management thinks that I knew all about your deal, but didn't say anything because we were fucking. That's what Larry David said to Ed. How could she be fucking the guy every night for two weeks and not know what's in his head? Those were his exact words. Ed didn't tell him we were together every night. Only two people knew that. Me and you. And I didn't say a word. That means that you did."

"Lucy, please..."

"You told your agent all about us and he told Larry. And now I'll probably lose my job. Thank you very fucking much, Calvin. This is proof that you can't go back in time without fucking up the future."

"What? Lucy, you're overreacting," I said. "Come on, let's forget this silly argument and go celebrate. I'll personally talk to Larry on Monday and straighten things out."

"No, I think I need to go," she said, holding up her hands to keep me away. She gazed into my eyes. "I wouldn't have said anything to anyone about your deal, Calvin. I would never do anything to hurt you. Obviously, that doesn't work both ways."

"Lucy, Jesus, come on..."

"Um, I need a little time to digest this," she said. "I'm going to stay at my place tonight."

"Okay, what about this weekend?"

She took a couple of steps back toward the door. "Um, I'm not sure."

"Lucy, you're being ridiculous," I said, rolling my eyes at her. "You realize that, right? You're overreacting. Don't leave. There's more I want to tell you. At least let me help you straighten things out."

"That's okay," she said, turning to leave. "I don't need your help. Not anymore."

And with that, she was gone, leaving me pissed off and confused. It wouldn't matter how successful or rich I became, I would never figure women out. Never. Not in a million years.

# CHAPTER SIXTEEN: Lucy

CALVIN—COLE—WAS PROBABLY right. Maybe I was overreacting, but goddammit when you've spent the last eighteen years of your life being lied to by one man, it did not make it any easier being lied to by another. If anything, my tolerance for bullshit was even less now. My fuse was much shorter.

Even though I could feel myself falling back in love with Cole, I would not put up with being lied to or manipulated, no matter how good the intention behind the lie or how amazing the makeup sex might be. I was through being lied to and through being made the fool by a man I thought had feelings for me.

Honestly, as I walked out of the building that night I didn't know if I'd ever want to see Cole Walker again. Or if he'd want to see me. Maybe Thomas Wolf was right. You can't go home again. And you can't rekindle an old flame without getting your fingers burned.

I DIDN'T LOSE MY JOB on Monday because the meeting with management never happened. Word came down from on high that morning that the meeting was canceled and there would be no need for further discussion. I asked Ed what happened and he just shrugged it off without speculation. Either management decided that I'd done nothing wrong or Cole had intervened on my behalf as he had said he would.

Either way, life moved on.

I sat at my desk staring at my phone that afternoon, contemplating calling him, but deciding against it. Call it silly human pride, but I had it set in my mind that if Cole wanted to makeup, he would have to call me and apologize for lying and beg me to take him back. If I called him, it would be as if I was the one crawling back begging for forgiveness. I had done a lifetime of crawling when I was married to Randy. Never was that going to happen again.

But Cole did not call that Monday afternoon.

Or the next.

Or the next.

According to the steady stream of press releases and *Entertainment Tonight* coverage about his new show, Dr. Cole Walker would be in Los Angeles for the next several months prepping for his new show that would premiere in the fall. I guess he had turned over all his patients to other doctors in his practice so he could focus on becoming the next Dr. Oz.

Sometimes, I'd find myself at my desk after the evening newscast, sitting alone after everyone else had gone home. My office was always dark except for a small lamp on the credenza and the glow of my computer screen. I would type his name into Google and read the latest news of his career. There were always photos, lots of photos, of the handsome star rubbing elbows and god knows what else with Hollywood starlets and TV personalities. There's a photo with Oprah. Another with Jimmy Kimmel. Another with Heidi Klum.

"Good for you, Calvin," I would say quietly as I wiped the tears from my eyes. I could tell by the look on his face that he was happy. How could he not be? His every dream was coming true.

IT WAS FINALLY THE weekend and I was so glad to have nothing to do but lounge around in my pajamas and not worry about work. I loved my job, but it was starting to wear me out. The schedule was brutal and dealing with Bryant had not gotten any easier. To the contrary, he seemed to blame me for Cole not signing on with WNN and went out of his way to be a total fucking asshole. Stephanie had also switched into bitch diva mode. I spent most of my time coddling their egos and trying to settle arguments between them. When they were not on set, they didn't speak to each other or to me.

There was also increasing pressure from Ed, who looked like he might have a heart attack at any moment. The show's ratings had dropped a full point since I'd taken over six weeks ago. It wasn't my fault, he said, the ratings always dipped in the fall, but he had to bitch at someone because management was bitching to him. He made it clear that if the ratings weren't good in ten months when my contract came up, my contract probably would not be renewed. All in all, it made for a very tough work environment that was making me old before my time.

Then my cell phone rang that Saturday afternoon as I lay on the couch watching *Sleepless in Seattle* for the hundredth time on DVD. I picked up my phone and glanced at the screen, but didn't recognize the number. I sat up and cleared my throat, then answered the phone.

"Is this Lucinda Rhodes?" The man's voice on the phone was deep, like one you'd hear on the radio.

"Who is this?" I asked.

"This is Harry Prescott, Miss Rhodes," he said. "Forgive me calling you on the weekend, but I didn't want to approach you at work."

I searched my brain for the name Harry Prescott, but came up blank. "I'm sorry, Mr. Prescott. Why are you calling?"

"Miss Rhodes, I'm the Vice President of Syndication at Kingston Television. I'd like to speak to you about becoming the executive producer of The Dr. Cole Walker Show."

# CHAPTER SEVENTEEN: Cole

"ARE YOU SURE SHE'S coming in?"

"Her plane landed last night and she spent the night in the room we booked for her at the Four Seasons." Harry didn't bother to look up from his cellphone, which was clutched between his hands with his thumbs tapping away. "Relax, Cole. Why are you so nervous?"

"I'm not nervous," I said, lying badly as I sat on the edge of the plush leather chair across the desk from him. "I just haven't spoken to her in six weeks and I'm not sure how she's going to react when she sees me."

"She'll probably run away in horror," he said with a smile. He sent the text message he'd been typing out and set his phone on the table. "Besides, she is not going to see you."

"What?" I blinked at him. "Of course, she will. I'm going to be in the meeting."

He set the phone aside and shook his head at me. "No, actually you're not."

"Wait, I don't understand."

Even though the show had my name on it, Harry was technically my boss as VP of Syndication. I could argue a point with him all day but I knew from experience, Harry's word was law.

He said, "I think it's better that you're not here. I'm not refereeing an intervention between the two of you, nor am I interested in taking part in some romantic reunion. You asked me to consider her for the EP job and that's what I'm doing. If she's qualified, she'll be seriously considered. If not, she won't be. It's as simple as that. Having you here would only confuse things. If you want to see her, do so later, at the Four Seasons."

"Fine," I said quietly, knowing that he was right. "Tell me again what she said on the phone."

"I've told you ten times already," he huffed.

"Tell me again."

"Fine. I told her that I wanted to talk to her about the EP position on your show and asked if she would like to fly out for an interview."

"But you did not tell her that I would be here."

"No."

"Did she ask?"

"Yes."

"And you said no."

"I said that you were not normally involved in the initial interviews, nor would you be part of this one."

"And she still agreed to come."

"Obviously."

"Did you tell her you were interviewing other candidates?" I asked. "So, she wouldn't expect anything?"

"I told her she was just one of a dozen candidates that were being interviewed for the job. She initially said she wasn't interested, but when I asked what she had to lose just by interviewing, she said what the hell." He swept his hands around the office. "And here we are. Waiting for her to arrive."

The intercom on the desk buzzed. "Mr. Prescott? Miss Rhodes is here."

"Okay, get out of here and let me do my job," Harry said, getting to his feet and straightening his tie. He glanced at the platinum Rolex on his wrist. "You're due onset. Go out my private exit. I'll call you as soon as my meeting with her is over."

"Okay, fine," I said, heading for the door. I opened the door and paused. "Harry, I really appreciate this."

"It's not a problem," he said forward to open the door for me. "Can I ask you one question, Cole?"

"Sure."

"Why go to all this trouble just to make up with her? Why not just show up at her door with a dozen roses and a giant apology?"

"I don't think I have anything to apologize for," I said seriously.

"Maybe not," he said, slapping me on the back as he ushered me out the door. "But that's really not the point now, is it."

# CHAPTER EIGHTEEN: Lucy

I WAS RELUCTANT AT first to even accept the offer to interview for the EP spot on Cole's show. I mean, come on, I knew I wasn't being asked to interview because of my experience or skills. I had produced live newscasts for years, but producing a recorded, one-hour talk show would be a whole different ballgame. Not to mention that I would be working with Cole again, a man I hadn't heard from in almost two months.

"I can assure you, Miss Rhodes, if you were not qualified to handle the job you and I would not be talking," Harry Prescott said in a tone that told me he wasn't bullshitting. He did not impress me as a bullshitter, or the kind of guy who would acquiesce to a request just to keep his talent happy, unlike me who had hired Bryant's niece as an assistant just to get him off my back.

He continued on, "Cole Walker is the talent, but Kingston Television owns the show. We would never hire someone based solely on a personal recommendation or a past relationship. So, the question is, do you want to fly to Los Angeles on Monday to chat with me in person or not?"

It took me less than two seconds to say yes, not just because I was interested in the job, but because I might see Cole again, even though Prescott made it clear that Cole would not be in the interview. I had cried myself to sleep many nights over the way things ended. At the very least, maybe this trip would give us the chance to just shake hands and put our relationship behind us once and for all.

HARRY PRESCOTT WAS tall and lanky and impeccably dressed in a tailored blue pinstripe suit and bright yellow tie. He was sitting behind a large mahogany desk in an office that made mine look like a broom closet. He came around the desk and warmly shook my hand, and directed me to sit in a red leather chair across the desk from him. As we settled in, the assistant who had escorted me back appeared again to set a silver tray on the desk that held two china cups and a silver coffee service and fixings. She poured two cups of coffee while Harry sat smiling at me, then she left the room.

"So, how was your flight?" he asked as he slid one cup toward me and picked up his own. "And how was the hotel?"

"The flight was fine and the Four Seasons is amazing, thank you," I said, picking up the coffee to drink it black. "I appreciate the gesture."

"The gesture?" he asked, his manicured gray eyebrows arching.

"I doubt you fly every candidate first class and put them up at the Four Seasons," I said. "That's all."

"Ah, you think that you are getting special treatment because you and Dr. Walker are old friends."

"Am I not?" I asked the question with an expectant smile. "Oh well, it was nice to feel special for a while."

"So, let's talk about your job at WNN," he said, setting the cup aside without ever drinking from it. He steepled his fingers and rested his chin on them. "Are you happy there?"

I took a careful sip of the steaming coffee and shrugged. "Happy enough, I suppose."

"If you were happy there, you wouldn't be here," he said, holding out his hands, smiling. "Unless you are here just out of curiosity, of course."

"Let's assume it's a little of both," I said. I glanced around the room. "Is Cole going to join us?"

"No, as I said over the phone, he is not involved in initial interviews," he said, picking up the cup again. He brought it to his lips and took a careful sip. "Can I be frank with you, Miss Rhodes?"

"Of course."

"You're here because Dr. Walker said you were an amazing EP and worthy of a conversation. However, the ultimate decision as to who is hired rests solely on me. So, let's just forget your relationship with Dr. Walker and conduct ourselves like two professionals who do not have him as a mutual acquaintance, because I assure you, I would never hire anyone simply because the talent suggested I do so. Are we clear?"

I smiled at him. I liked this guy. He reminded me of a tall, skinny Ed. I said, "Clear as a bell, Mr. Prescott. I would love to forget that I know Cole Walker, I mean, for the sake of this interview."

"Good," he said, rubbing his hands together. "Let's start again..."

THE INTERVIEW LASTED less than an hour. Prescott had a copy of my resume and he spent most of that time staring at it and asking me inane questions about my career. I got the feeling that it wasn't really an interview at all. It was just Prescott going through the motions so he could report back to Cole that he had indeed interviewed me as promised, and could now mark me off the list.

I left feeling a little dazed and confused. I didn't get to see Cole, nor did I have a clue if I really had a shot at the job. Hell, I didn't even know if I wanted the job. Would I take it if it were offered to me? I honestly did not know.

I didn't even bother going back to the Four Seasons to check out. I had a sneaking suspicion that things might turn out this way, so I had brought my bag with me.

I caught a cab to the airport and switched my ticket to an earlier flight. Ten hours later, I was back home. Life goes on.

# CHAPTER NINETEEN: Lucy

A WEEK PASSED WITHOUT word from Harry Prescott regarding the EP job on the *Dr. Cole Walker Show*. I figured it was for the best anyway, and quickly dismissed thoughts of the job from my mind and focused on the job I already had.

I was a little pissed off, feeling like a pawn in a chess match between Prescott and Cole, but I was also a little curious as to why Cole didn't just call and apologize. I mean, wasn't that what the interview was really about? Getting me to L.A. so he could apologize for being a lying asshole and we could pick up where we left off?

Or was I being too presumptuous?

Maybe Cole wasn't interested in me anymore.

Maybe the interview was meant as Cole's parting gift to me for playing and losing his game. I fucked you over, but hey, at least I got you an interview. Asshole.

"OKAY, GREAT SHOW EVERYBODY," I said, pressing the console button so everyone could hear my voice through their earpieces and headsets. "Have a great weekend."

I took off the headset and mussed my hair as I watched the set go dark on the monitors and waited for everyone to turn off the controls and computers and exit the control room. I liked to be the last one to leave the room, just to make sure everything was switched off and put to bed. Plus, it kept me from having to make small talk in the hallway back to my office. I wasn't trying to be antisocial, I just didn't feel like talking. I glanced around at the blinking lights and switches, then shut off the overhead lights and went out the door.

I went down the stairs to my office to gather up my things. I was standing behind my desk shoving my laptop into the computer bag when I heard a tap on the door. I looked up to see someone holding a dozen roses in front of their face. When his blue eyes appeared from over the top of the bouquet, I felt my heart jump in my chest.

"Cole? What are you doing here?"

"Following a friend's advice," he said, coming into the room with the flowers at arm's length, as if he were afraid to get too close too soon. "Can we talk, Lucy?"

"Sure," I said, taking the flowers and holding them to my nose. They smelled wonderful. I blinked at him. "I don't guess you're here to tell me I got the job."

"No, I'm afraid not," he said with a sad face. He took off his overcoat and hung it on a rack by the door. "They chose Oprah's former EP. Nice woman. Bit bossy, but that's what it takes to keep me in line."

"Wow, hard to compete with that," I said. "So, why are you here?"

Cole took a deep breath and stared into my eyes. It was hard for me not to jump into his arms. He pressed his hands down on the back of the chair across the desk and worked up an apologetic smile.

"I wanted to apologize," he said quietly. "And to let you know that I'll be moving to Los Angeles next week."

"Permanently?" The word tasted bitter on my tongue.

"Yeah," he said, head shaking. "Permanently."

"Oh."

"And I was hoping you would come with me."

I blinked at him for a moment, unsure that I'd heard the words correctly. I set the flowers on the credenza behind my desk and lowered myself into the chair. My head was suddenly swimming and my knees felt weak. This, I was not expecting, at all.

# CHAPTER TWENTY: Cole

THE COLOR DRAINED FROM Lucy's face and she sat down in the chair behind her desk. "Lucy, are you okay?" I asked, reaching out for her. "Do you need a water or anything?"

"Um, I need you to sit," she said, waving a hand at the chair I was leaning on. "Then say all that again."

I sat down on the edge of the chair and set my arms on the edge of the desk. "I said I was moving to L.A. and I want you to come with me."

"Move to L.A. with you?" She spoke like she was drugged or something. "Are you crazy? I haven't seen or heard from you in almost two months, and you show up today asking me to move across country with you? You're nuts. I mean, you have to be absolute nuts."

I smiled and held out my hands across the desk. "Yeah, I mean, I know this is all very sudden, but..."

"I haven't heard that apology," she said quietly. She leaned back in the chair and wrapped her arms around herself. "Before we even talk about moving to Los Angeles, I need to hear you say you're sorry."

Women. Go figure. I took a deep breath and granted her wish.

"I am sorry, Lucy. I should have told you about the syndication deal, but my agent ordered me not to. It wasn't that I didn't trust you, it was that they didn't trust anyone. I mean, the deal was worth millions of dollars. But that's no excuse. I'm sorry I didn't tell you and I'm sorry your feelings got hurt. I'd never hurt you, Lucy, not on purpose. You know that."

"Do I?"

"I hope so."

"And I'm just supposed to forgive you? Just like that?"

I gave her my best smile. "Again, I hope so."

"I'm not sure it's that easy," she said, leaning forward with her arms still wound tightly around her. "You have to prove to me that I can trust you again."

"You can trust me, Lucy," I said, giving her a playful frown. "I'm a doctor. *And* I play one on TV."

"Shut up," she said, giggling as the ice in her heart began to melt. "You can't lie to me ever again, Calvin. I just can't take being lied to. I've had my fill of it."

"I will do whatever it takes to prove that you can trust me," I said. I gave her a dreamy look and wiggled my fingers. "Now, can we talk about L.A.?"

"In a minute," she said. She leaned back and started unbuttoning her blouse. "First, close and lock that fucking door."

# EPILOG: Lucy

HOW COULD I DO THIS. Forgive a man who had costed me my job. Literally.

But that man was all that mattered to me.

And being with him was all I could care about.

Why was forgiving him so easy? Probably because I was so ready for it. I was waiting for him to just say it, and the moment he said it, I showed him how ready I was.

It was no wonder Los Angeles and New York were on opposite sides of the country because the two cities could not have been more different.

New York prided itself on being the city that never slept. It was also a city that could overwhelm and assault your senses in more ways than one. New York was home to the world's finest restaurants, theaters, museums, art galleries, and cultural centers. It was also freakin' loud and noisy and hectic and full of assholes and garbage and stank to high heaven.

Los Angeles, on the other hand, was much more spread out and less cramped, but it had terrible traffic at rush hour, more than its share of assholes, and sometimes you could literally see the air in front of your face. Still, Los Angeles was home now. I'd make the best of it. Which wasn't hard to do living in a Bel Air mansion with the hottest new star on TV.

Cole's show had been syndicated in a hundred markets and was a bonafide ratings hit. It quickly went to number one in its time slot in major markets and new affiliates were signing on every day. *Entertainment Tonight* called Cole the best thing to hit TV since Dr. Oz and Dr. Phil. Thankfully, Cole's ego wasn't so big that he bought into the hype. He knew how bright his star was and how quickly it was rising. He also knew how quickly stars could fall to the ground. Maybe that's why he got nervous sometimes before the cameras rolled. I found it hilarious that a guy who could literally take out, repair, and replace a human heart got nervous being on TV. I also found it incredibly cute.

We had been in L.A. for just over a month and were still settling into the new house, which was provided as part of Cole's contract with Kingston TV. I had landed a job with the local CBS station in L.A., producing the noon newscast Monday through Friday. I went to work at eight and came home at five. The salary was less than a third of what I'd been making at WNN, but the bullshit I had to put up with, and the stress it caused, was slashed by ninety-nine percent. Money wasn't everything to me. Of course, that was easy to say when your significant other was a multimillionaire.

Funny, that term "significant other".

Cole and I loved each other deeply and had said the "L" word, but we still didn't know how to refer to each other out in public. Were we boyfriend and girlfriend? Significant others? Partners in crime? Was he my man and was I his lady? Or were we just two old flames that had reunited to cause one hell of a bonfire?

"YOUR DRINK, MADAM," Cole said as he came through the French doors with a mimosa in each hand. The pool area behind our house was totally secluded, which was why we never bothered to wear bathing suits when we lounged around the pool. I was lying naked on a lounge chair, my body slathered in sunscreen and still turning the color of honey.

I got up on my elbows and watched as Cole approached. He was also naked, muscles all sweaty and deeply tanned. His long cock swung from side to side as he came toward me. I licked my lips in anticipation of the cold drink and the hot cock.

"Thanks," I said, sitting up in the chair to take the drink. The sweat streamed down between my tits, sluicing toward my shaved cunt. I smiled when it slid over my clit, knowing that Cole loved the taste of a salty pussy.

I took a long sip and smacked my lips. "That's so good."

Cole sat down on the lounge chair next to me and sighed. I watched the muscles ripple through his body as he settled in. He was covered in a layer of oil and sweat. His skin glowed brown and red from the sun. His cock was draped over his thigh, moist with sweat, like a sausage sizzling on the grill.

"This is the life," he said, setting the drink on the glass table between our chairs. He lay flat with his hands behind his head and his eyes closed. He sighed heavily after a moment, as if he were falling asleep. He didn't open his eyes when he felt my fingers closing around his cock. He just sighed again and smiled.

"What are you doing?" he asked as his cock hardened in my hand, growing before my eyes. I slowly stroked his cock as the skin tightened around the shaft as it grew to full length and the head blossomed like a mushroom. I could feel the hot juices already pouring from my pussy, mixing with the sweat and sunscreen to lubricate my hole Cole's entry.

"I'm reliving the night we popped each other's cherries," I said, getting up to straddle his cock without ever letting him go. "Do you remember that night?" I swirled the head of his cock around my hole and let it slip inside. "Your cock was so big I thought you were going to split me open."

"I remember," he said, bringing his hands to my hips to steady me as I lowered my pussy onto his thick cock. I could feel my pussy closing around him. "Your pussy was so tight I didn't think I would get inside you. Just like now. God, you're so fucking tight, Lucy..."

"Do you remember the tip of your cock hitting my hymen, then breaking through?" I put my hands on his chest and squeezed his nipples as I slid my hips up and down the length of his cock that would fit inside me. Sweat dripped down my nose onto his chest. My body was already burning up on the outside. Now, the inside ignited to catch up.

"I remember the scent of your pussy," he said, breathlessly. "I could taste you on my tongue. I could smell you for days. My old man was furious that he couldn't get the smell out of the car, but I fucking loved it. Your pussy walls seemed to grip my cock like a thousand little fingers."

"Oh... fuck..." I moaned as he slid in and out. "God... I love fucking you..."

"And I love fucking you," he said. His fingers dug into my sides and he started lifting me up and down. "Now, fuck me faster."

I took a deep breath and started pummeling my cunt down on his cock. I could feel him hitting my cervix. Fuck, it was almost like I could feel him in my throat. The orgasm came quickly. My body was tingling from head to toe. My big tits swayed on my chest. Cole leaned up to take a hard nipple between his teeth and growled like a wild animal.

"Fuck... Cole... I'm cumming...holy fucking god... Cole... cum with me... cum with me now..."

I don't know how he did it, but Cole could literally cum on demand. He tightened his grip on my hips and pushed me down hard, filling every inch of me with his manhood. I felt his hot milk flowing within me as my juices washed down over his cock and balls. We jerked and grunted and moaned for a moment, then his grip on my hips loosened and I opened my eyes to see him smiling up at me.

"Just like that night," he said with a smile.

"Better," I said, my tongue hanging out. "I love you, Calvin Walker."

"I love you back, Lucy Walsh."

"Walker and Walsh," I said with a grin. "We never got to be side by side in the yearbook like you said."

"Is that your only regret?" he asked with a tentative smile.

"It is today," I said, leaning down to kiss him. "It is today."

**THE END**

# Don't miss out!

Visit the website below and you can sign up to receive emails whenever Amy Brent publishes a new book. There's no charge and no obligation.

https://books2read.com/r/B-A-GACH-EIPMB

BOOKS 2 READ

Connecting independent readers to independent writers.

Did you love *Filthy Doctor*? Then you should read *Filthy Professor*[1] by Amy Brent!

[2]

That's it, I can't stand it anymore! I've spent months trying to get Professor Logan Clark to notice me. I dress sexy, I gaze into his eyes, I lick my lips when he looks at me. I want to get him out of his classroom and out of his clothes for a little private, one-on-one tutoring...

COURTNEY SHAW: I'm a smoking hot red head with a sex drive that would make a porn star blush and a major daddy complex. Older men are my thing, and lots of them have sampled the sweet treats I have in my panties. So why isn't Logan Clark jumping at the chance to be with me? Even after our little oral exam in the restroom he keeps pushing me away. Is this his idea of torture? Well, two can play at that game...

---

1. https://books2read.com/u/4DgL0r
2. https://books2read.com/u/4DgL0r

LOGAN CLARK: Damn this girl, doesn't she understand that there are rules against professors having sex with students, no matter how smoking hot and sexy they are? She doesn't seem to care that screwing her could get me fired. I'm not going to risk my job just to have sex with her. No way. Not even after she drops a wet thong on my desk and shows up naked at my door. I've worked too hard to get where I am at this school. I'm not going blow it all for her. At least that's what I keep telling myself...

# Also by Amy Brent

**Filthy**

Filthy Boss

Filthy Doctor

Filthy Professor

Filthy Seal

Filthy Cowboy

Filthy Daddy

Filthy Coach

**Forbidded**

The Doctor's Fake Marriage

**Forbidden**

Fake Fiance

One More Chance

Crave Me

My Best Friend's Dad

The Doctor's Fake Marriage

Dad's Best Friend

**Forbidden Fantasies**
Daddy's Business Partner
Daddy's Friend
Daddy O
Climbing His Corporate Ladder
Taken By Daddy's Boss
Filthy Liar

**Standalone**
Teachers' Pet
Filthy Box Set
Knocked Up By My Brother's Best Friend
My Best Friend's Brother
My Best Friend's Ex
Say You're Mine
Club Desire Box Set
My Boyfriend's Dad
Fighting For Her
Forbidden Love Box Set
Love Undercover
Friends With Benefits
A Royal Menage
Baby Fever
Vegas Baby
Brother's Best Friend for Christmas
Christmas With My Best Friend's Dad
My Son's Sitter
Single Dad's Christmas Present
Surrendering To 3 Alphas

Because I Love You
Catching Up With Daddy
Claiming Cinderella
Double Trouble
First Love
First Time
Knocked Up By My Brother's Best Friend
My Best Friend's Boyfriend
Pretend Daddy
Redemption
Roomies With Benefits
Royally Yours
Rub Me The Right Way
Show Stopper
That One Night
The Baby Contract
Truth Or Dare
Santa's Naughty List
Quickie on Christmas
Con Man

www.ingramcontent.com/pod-product-compliance
Ingram Content Group UK Ltd.
Pitfield, Milton Keynes, MK11 3LW, UK
UKHW021657190726
13853UKWH00001B/308